## Books 1-3

### Amy Tree

*Illustrated by Gwen Millward*

Orion
Children's Books

First published in Great Britain in 2010
by Orion Children's Books
a division of the Orion Publishing Group Ltd
Orion House
5 Upper St Martin's Lane
London WC2H 9EA

An Hachette UK Company

1 3 5 7 9 8 6 4 2

Text copyright © Amy Tree
*The Queen's Bracelet* 2008
*The Silver Pool* 2008
*The Dragon's Revenge* 2008
Illustrations copyright © Gwen Millward
*The Queen's Bracelet* 2008
*The Silver Pool* 2008
*The Dragon's Revenge* 2008

The Orion Publishing Group's policy is to use papers that are natural,
renewable and recyclable products and made from wood grown in sustainable
forests. The logging and manufacturing processes are expected to conform to
the environmental regulations of the country of origin.

A catalogue record for this book is available from the British Library.

ISBN 978 1 4440 0103 7

Printed and bound in the UK by
CPI Mackays, Chatham ME5 8TD

www.orionbooks.co.uk
www.charmseekers.co.uk

# CONTENTS

# The Thirteen Charms of Karisma

When Charm became queen of Karisma, the wise and beautiful Silversmith made her a precious gift. It was a bracelet. On it were fastened thirteen silver amulets, which the Silversmith called 'charms', in honour of the new queen.

It was part of Karisma law. Whenever there was a new ruler, the Silversmith made a special gift, to help them care for the world they had inherited. And this time it was a bracelet. She told Queen Charm it was magical because the charms held the power to control the forces of nature and keep everything in balance. She must take the greatest care of them. As long as she, and she alone, had possession of the charms, all would be well.

And so it was, until the bracelet was stolen by a spider, and fell into the hands of Zorgan, the magician. Then there was chaos!

# the Queen's Bracelet

*For Norah Adams*
*— A life lived to the full to the very end.*

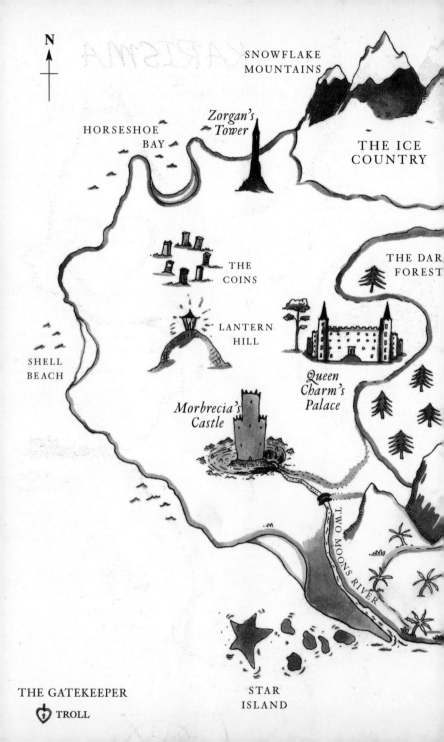

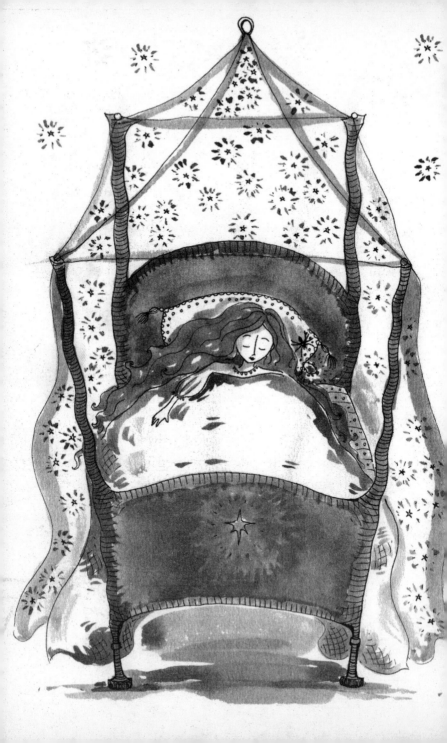

# One

The two moons of Karisma shone brightly over the palace. Inside, Queen Charm slept peacefully, unaware of the enormous spider crawling over her bed.

The young queen had placed her charm bracelet under the pillow for safe-keeping. She had been warned to take care of it. And she did. So long as she had the bracelet, all would be well. The Silversmith had made that very clear. But should it fall into the wrong hands . . .

The spider moved swiftly. Silently it scuttled under the snow-white pillow, gripped its prize and eased the bracelet out. Thirteen silver charms glinted in the moonlight.

"Got it!" said the spider, Morbrecia. "Mine at last!"

The Silversmith wakes with a start.

"Something is wrong!" she tells herself.

She senses evil in the air. If the worst has happened . . . if, as she fears, the charm bracelet has fallen into the wrong hands . . . there will be consequences. Karisma will change. The laws of nature, so carefully held in balance by the magical bracelet, will fall apart.

"Hushish!* This is a bad business!"

Her sense of foreboding persists. It grips like a vice, tighter and tighter, until she is convinced the bracelet has been stolen. Who by? She has her suspicions. And, if she's right, it won't be easy getting it back!

She throws off the coverlet. Her gossamer robe shimmers like a shower of stars, as she crosses the room, to sit at her dressing table. A look of anxiety clouds her face. She brushes her hair vigorously, as if to rid herself of these terrible thoughts. She will go to the palace first thing in the morning to see Charm.

But first she must find someone to help look for what is lost. A seeker who will search far and wide. One who will care enough to carry out this quest and not give up, no matter what dangers lie ahead.

She rises and goes to the window, flings it wide

* * * * * * * * * * * * * * * * * * * * * * * * * *

✱ **Hushish** – a word used to express dismay

16

to breathe the chill night air. She gazes in wonder at the two moons casting their silvery-blue light – there's such a strange aura about them tonight! – and, away across the heavens, to the brightly shining Outworld . . .⋆

\* \* \* \* \* \* \* \* \* \* \* \* \* \* \* \* \* \* \* \* \* \* \* \* \*

⋆ **Outworld** – the name Karismans call our world

17

"Quisto!"* she exclaims. "The box! How could I forget!"

How indeed! She recalls transporting herself to the Outworld to place a special box there. Few possess the magic power to 'transworld', as it is known, and even she had done so only once – to accomplish a secret mission. With her gift of foresight, she had predicted the box would serve a purpose in the Outworld, at some time in the future. Now it seems that the time has come.

The Silversmith closes her eyes, snaps her fingers, *click*! She's in a trance, 'seeing' far, far beyond the boundaries of Karisma. Who has the box? Who? Ah, yes! She breathes a sigh of relief. It's someone very special . . .

She has found her seeker!

* * * * * * * * * * * * * * * * * * * * * * * * * * * * * *

★ **Quisto** – an exclamation of surprise

# Two

Sesame Brown was munching a mouthful of muesli when she exploded.

"Dad! Did you know orangutans in Borneo are starving?"

A pumpkin seed flew across the breakfast table. It landed near her dad, Nic Brown, who was sitting opposite.

"Uh-huh," mumbled Nic, brushing the stray seed aside. He flicked through the pages of his newspaper. "It's here somewhere . . ."

Sesame looked up from reading *Wild About Wildlife* on the back of the cereal packet. She rolled her eyes.

"Dad, are you listening? This is serious!"

Nic put down his paper. Sesame was so like her mum, Poppy. She had Poppy's big brown eyes and Nic loved the way they flew wide open when she was cross. Like now.

Sesame went on reading.

"The rainforest which is their natural habitat is being cut down by unscru . . . un-*scrooo*-pu . . . "

"Unscrupulous?" offered Nic.

"Yes," said Sesame. "*Unscrupulous* timber operators, to clear the way for palm oil crops. The orangutans have no food and nowhere to live."

"How awful," said Nic, sneaking another look at his paper.

"AND," said Sesame, banging her spoon on the table to emphasise the point, "if something isn't done about it soon, wild orangutans will become EXTINCT!"

"Terrible!" agreed Nic.

The sudden *BANG* made him jump. He decided to give Sesame his full attention.

Again Nic was reminded of Poppy. She would have been as concerned about the orangutans as their daughter was now. And, when Sesame took an interest in something, she made it her business to find out all about it!

Poppy Brown had died in a car accident when Sesame was a baby. She had been a journalist, writing about the environment, climate change and things

20

like that. And, like Sesame, she was crazy about animals — wild ones, tame ones, anything with whiskers, paws or claws. Not to mention ponies! Sesame was pony-mad too.

Just then Sesame's two little kittens, Chips and Pins, scampered across the floor.

"Oooo! Come here," she said, scooping them up and giving them a cuddle. The plight of the orangutan, it seemed, had been temporarily forgotten.

While Sesame stroked the kittens, Nic picked up his newspaper again. He found the photograph he was looking for.

"Look, Ses," he said. "Here's one of mine."

Nic was a photographer for THE DAILY TIMES. He was always rushing off to cover a news story. Sometimes, at weekends or in the holidays, he took Sesame with him.

Carefully, Sesame unhooked herself from the kittens' claws, and put them down to play. Then she looked at the picture. Three glamorous models wearing swirly skirts, tops and jackets were posing outside a new shop. **TIP TOPS** had just opened on the High Street.

"Oh Dad! Why didn't you take ME?" she wailed.

Sesame and her friend, Maddy, were seriously into fashion. "Tip Tops looks cooool!"

"Because I was there yesterday while you were at scho-o-o-o-o-l," he said.

"But today is Saturday!" said Sesame. "Can I go shopping with Maddy, Dad? PLEASE!"

"Ok," said Nic. "But don't stay out too long. I'm covering a football match this afternoon. But Lossy will be here, when you get back."

Lossy was Sesame's gran. Her real name was Lois, but when Sesame was little she'd called her Lossy and the name had stuck ever since. Sesame loved Lossy. Whenever her dad had to be away for work, Lossy was always there.

"Yippee!" sang Sesame, dancing round the kitchen. Chips and Pins thought this was a new game and pounced on her slippers.

"Ouch!" she squealed. "You've got sharp little claws!"

She ran upstairs to her room. It was right at the top of the house with low, sloping ceilings and a window. The walls were covered with Sesame's drawings (mostly ponies) and pictures of wild animals (mostly orangutans). And there was stuff all over the floor.

But Sesame liked it that way and knew where everything was. She skilfully hopped around a stack of CDs, two tops, a half-finished bead bangle, magazines and a pair of jelly pumps, to put on a CD. It was her favourite band, Crystal Chix. She sang

along while sweeping her long brown hair back with a hairband. Then she went to look in her wardrobe.

"What AM I going to wear?" She said with a sigh, staring at the jumble of clothes.

But it didn't take her long to choose a green stripy top to go with her jeans and funky trainers. After dressing in double-quick time, she grabbed her mobile and sat beside her bed. Her teddy Alfie flopped sideways on to the pillow. Propping him up again, Sesame kissed his nose and switched on her mobile. She sent a text to Maddy:

A few minutes later, Maddy replied:

C U AT TIP
TOPS AT 10.
DNT B L8!
LOL SESAME
MWAH MWAH :)

GR8 C U
LUV MADDY
XX :)

"Great!" cried Sesame, jumping up and slinging a large bag over her shoulder as she went out.

She was halfway through the door, when she remembered her necklace. It was one she often wore – a silver chain and locket, with tiny pictures of her parents inside. It meant a lot to Sesame. She kept it on her bedside table with some family photographs and a jewellery box, which had once belonged to her mum.

When Poppy died, Nic had given the jewellery box to Sesame. The lid was beautifully painted, with some strange symbols round a circle. Sesame was sure they were some sort of code.

Once she'd asked her dad about it, but Nic had only shrugged and said, "No idea, Ses. I found that box in a junk shop. Just thought it looked special. I gave it to your mum when you were born. She loved it."

"So do I," Sesame told him. "But I wish I knew what those symbols meant."

"Well, knowing you," Nic had said, "you won't give up till you do!"

Sesame had pretended to peer at the lid through a magnifying glass, like a detective.

"Sesame Brown will track it down!" she'd said.

And they'd laughed.

Sesame picked up her necklace. It felt curiously warm, as if it had just been held. When she fastened the clasp, there was a tingle at the nape of her neck. She ran out of her room and down the stairs, two at a time. She found Nic checking his camera, ready for work.

"What time will you be home?" she asked.

"Sometime this evening," said Nic. "It's a late kick-off. I'll see you and Lossy later.

"Ok," she said, giving him a quick kiss. "Love you. Bye!"

Sesame walked along the pavement towards the High Street. Her best friend, Maddy Webb, lived on the other side of town and Sesame wished she lived closer. They did absolutely everything together.

At **TIP TOPS** Sesame checked her watch. Ten o'clock on the dot. She liked to be on time. She looked around for Maddy but she wasn't there. Surprise surprise, thought Sesame. Maddy was nearly always late!

There were lots of girls hurrying into the shop and Sesame longed to join them. Just then, she spotted Liz and Gemma. They saw her and came over.

"Hi, Sesame!" said Liz.

"Waiting for Maddy?" asked Gemma.

"Yeah," said Sesame. "We arranged to meet at ten. But you know Maddy!"

"Mmm!" said Liz, with a knowing grin.

"She's probably forgotten something and had to go back for it," said Gemma. "Maddy's SO forgetful!"

They all laughed, then Liz and Gemma went into **TIP TOPS** leaving Sesame to wait outside.

Sometimes Sesame got cross with Maddy for being late. Then they would fall out. But because they were best friends it never lasted for long. Maddy always said she was sorry, and they made up.

While she was waiting, Sesame looked in the window. There were some fabulous clothes! But one top seemed to stand out from all the rest. It was bright red with a sparkling heart.

She simply couldn't stop looking at it. And the more she looked, the more the heart seemed to . . . beat. Yes, beat! She was sure of it. How weird, thought Sesame.

The colours began to swirl. Round and round, faster and faster, until Sesame felt herself floating. And suddenly she floated right through the heart, into a silvery mist . . .

# Three

The scream from Queen Charm's bedroom was shrill. It could be heard throughout the palace. The piercing screech startled one sleepy guard wide-awake. Officer Dork raced to the royal apartment and found the queen in a state of shock. Her maid, Ozina, was trying to comfort her.

"What happened?" she asked.

"It was ghastly!" said Charm. "I thought I was dreaming. Something was crawling. Ugh! I saw, I'm sure I saw . . ."

She wasn't making much sense.

"Go on," said Ozina gently.

Dork stepped closer, to hear.

"A sp-sp-spider!" stuttered Charm. "An ENORMOUS spider. And it was stealing the bracelet!"

"Eeek!" squealed Ozina, jumping onto the bed. She was afraid the spider might still be on the floor. "I hate spiders!"

Dork rolled his eyes. Girls, eh! He thought the queen had probably imagined it all. She'd had a nightmare. Yes, that was it. But he managed to look

concerned as he asked:

"You say the intruder was a spider, Your Majesty?"

"Yes," said Charm. "A spider. But never mind that now. It's the BRACELET that matters!"

Both Dork and Ozina knew how important the bracelet was. Everyone in Karisma knew about the bracelet, with its thirteen lucky charms. So if it had been stolen . . .

Ozina peeped under the pillow. She knew Charm put the bracelet there every night. And, sure enough, it was missing.

With her mind now focused on the bracelet,

Charm regained her regal composure.
Dork knew better than to underestimate
this young and beautiful queen, for her
fine, slender features concealed hidden
strengths. Charm took her duties seriously
and ruled her people well.

Dork stood smartly to attention, awaiting orders.
He watched Charm cross the room to the window, to
look out at the starry sky. Caught in the moonlight,
her long, fair hair looked like a silvery waterfall,
falling to her waist. How unlike her sister,
Morbrecia, he thought. And an
image of Morbrecia, with her
wild, jet black hair and
eyes, dark as the night,
filled his head. He was in
awe of Morbrecia. And
just a little bit afraid . . .

His thoughts were
interrupted by a courteous
but firm command. Charm
had turned to face him,
clear what must be done.

"Officer Dork," she
said. "Take a search
party and find my
bracelet. I must
have it back!"

## Four

Sesame landed with a *THUMP*! She found herself sprawling on a patch of purple moss, staring at two large, hairy feet.

"Who are YOU?" said a voice, from somewhere not very far above her head.

Sesame looked up. A troll was standing near the twisted trunk of a tree, looking very surprised.

"Er . . . Sesame Brown," said Sesame, in a daze. She sat up, at eye-level with the troll, who was peering at her intensely through bushy eyebrows.

"You're from the Outworld, aren't you?" he said. Then he leaned a little closer to say, "I've heard all about you Outworlders! But I never thought I'd meet one. Why did you come?"

"What?" asked Sesame.

"The precise nature of your visit?" said the troll, a little irritably. "In other words, what . . . are . . . you doing . . . here?" He said it slowly, as if Sesame was stupid.

"I haven't a clue," she said. Which was true. "Anyway, who are you? Where am I?"

"Tssh!" muttered the troll. "You don't know much, do you? I'm Gatekeeper One. And you've just barged into Karisma."

"Gatekeeper? Kar-is-ma? Where's that?"

Sesame was utterly bewildered, though she was beginning to remember being whisked off her feet and spun round, like clothes in a washing machine. There were so many questions she wanted to ask but she found herself saying:

"How many gates are there?"

"Twelve, of course," said the troll. "Twelve gates. Twelve gatekeepers." Then he added with a grin: "Lucky you came through mine. I'm one of the nice ones. Get it? ONE of the nice ones!"

"Y-e-e-e-s," said Sesame. It was obviously one of his favourite jokes. "And the others?" she asked, curious to know about those, too.

"You don't want to tangle with some of them!" said the troll, wiping a hairy hand across his brow. "Let me see. There's a one-eyed giant at number Four. Foul temper he's got. And the monster at number Eleven likes to eat his visitors. He calls them . . . his elevenses!"

And suddenly he burst out laughing.

Tears rolled down his cheeks and his belly shook. Sesame giggled nervously.

Eventually, the gatekeeper stopped laughing and gave her a map. He stamped it with the words:

## Outworlder - Tourist

He handed it to her saying:

"Map of Karisma. Gate closes at sunset. Don't be late and watch out for gribblers!"

"What are gribblers?" asked Sesame, taking a quick look over her shoulder. There was no reply. The gate-keeper had disappeared. He'd simply vanished.

"Huh! He wasn't very helpful!" said Sesame, nervously fiddling with her necklace. The locket suddenly sprang open and there were the tiny pictures of her parents, smiling back at her. Seeing her dad and her mum made her feel much better.

"Right," she said decisively, snapping the locket shut and opening the map. "Karisma, here I come! But I hope I don't meet any gribblers, whatever they are!"

As she wandered slowly along a narrow path, Sesame looked at the map. She reckoned she was in the Dark Forest, which was clearly marked. She could also make out a speck of light on the map. It appeared to be moving in the direction she was going. To try it out, she zigzagged across the path and, sure enough, the light tracked her movements exactly.

"Cool!" said Sesame. "A magic map!"

Now she looked around, fascinated by everything she saw. Creepers grew before her eyes, coiling long tentacles round trees, like snakes; jagged shoots shot up through the undergrowth; bare bushes suddenly burst into leaf. The forest was alive! It seemed everything was waking up to the early morning sunlight, filtering through the branches.

And the air was full of sounds. As Sesame went deeper into the forest, she heard the hollow knocking of a beak on wood; the noisy chatter of unseen birds; the *whoop-whoop!* call of a strange animal; the crackle of shrivelled leaves underfoot . . .

Sesame had just stopped to take a look at a gigantic tree with blue spotted leaves, when *Whoop-whoop! Whoop-whoop!* Something with spiky pink fur crashed down from above.

Terrified, Sesame jumped back.

"Are you a gri-gri–gribbler?" she asked.

But the creature, which had landed at her feet, just stared at her with its big round eyes. They looked sad. *Whoop-whoooo!* it cried, in a pitiful way. And Sesame immediately felt sorry for it.

"Oh, you poor thing!" she said. "I don't care even if you ARE a gribbler. You look like a baby who's lost its mother. I'll help you, if I can. My name's Sesame," she said. "What's yours?"

"Fig," said Fig, who had just learnt to say his name and liked the sound of it.

"Well, come on, Fig, let's go and find your mother!" she said.

And Fig *whooped* and looked much happier.

The two set off together through the forest, with Fig holding tight to Sesame's hand. Fig seemed to trust her completely, which made Sesame feel very responsible. Besides, she loved a challenge! Sesame Brown was never happier than when she was solving a problem.

Glancing at the map to see where they were, she now saw *two* specks of light — one slightly bigger than the other.

"Look," she said to Fig, "that's us. And there's a palace!"

Sesame clambered on to a rock, to get a better view. There! She could just make out the palace in the distance, with the sun glinting on its towers. She had a good look round for Fig's mother too. Disappointingly, there wasn't another pink creature in sight. But she was curious to see a group of soldiers in smart red and gold uniforms, nearby. They appeared to be searching for something too. Some were crawling over tangled roots, while others peered into bushes.

Sesame jumped off the rock. One of the soldiers spotted her and stepped forward. It was Dork. He eyed Sesame suspiciously. She's not from these parts! he thought.

"Name?" Dork barked the question.

And when Sesame told him, Dork asked her sarcastically:

"Looking for something, Sesame Brown?"

"Yes!" said Sesame, eagerly. She thought the soldier might help. "Fig has lost its mother. Have you seen any of . . . these? Do you know what they're called?"

Dork knew very well.

"Tunganoras," he said, dismissively. "We get a lot of them round here. But I've got more important things to do. I suppose you and your furry friend haven't, by any chance, come across a bracelet?"

"No," said Sesame. "Have you lost one?"

"*I* haven't," said Dork, "but Queen Charm has.

Her Majesty's charm bracelet was stolen last night."

"Oh dear!" said Sesame. But an exciting idea had just whizzed into her head. Supposing *I* could be the one to find the queen's bracelet? Wow! Maybe that's why I'm here? "Leave it to me," she said, helpfully. "Sesame Brown will track it down!" And she meant every word.

But Dork thought she was joking and was in no mood for funny remarks.

"Queen Charm's bracelet is a bit special," he said briskly. "It must be found and returned as soon as possible!"

"Right!" said Sesame. "I'll do my best. Any idea who stole it?"

Dork looked uneasy.

"It was stolen by a spider," he said quietly. "A whopping great SPIDER!"

38

# Five

The soaring column of black rock, which was Zorgan's Tower, rose from the barren landscape, like a cobra ready to strike. From his Star Room, high at the top, the magician used a powerful telescope to study the heavens above – and spy on people below.

It was here the sorcerer waited impatiently for Morbrecia to return. He paced round and round, fiddling with a gold medallion. Rings glittered on every finger. Zorgan loved bright things. And soon he would have Charm's exquisite bracelet to add to his collection. He was beside himself with anticipation!

To pass the time, he amused himself remembering how this had all come about. It had been so easy persuading Morbrecia to fall in with his plans. And, as for turning her into a spider . . . Morbrecia had loved that!

A spider stealing from her sister who was terrified of creepy-crawlies. Vixee!★

* * * * * * * * * * * * * * * * * * * * * * * * * *

★ **Vixee** – a gleeful, triumphant exclamation meaning great or wicked

Suddenly, Zorgan's thoughts were interrupted. Something was being dragged slowly across the floor. He listened and looked down. There she was!

Zorgan smirked. Morbrecia trusted him completely. "I'll make you greater than Queen Charm," he had promised. "Bring me the bracelet and I'll empower it with dark magic – SO much more dangerous and exciting! You'll have such fun creating havoc and mayhem!"

A likely story! Zorgan intended to keep it for himself. The Silversmith had cast each lovely charm. They had special powers. Besides, the bracelet was fabulous! It was only right HE should be the one to wear it. Zorgan stretched out his hand . . .

"Not so fast!" said Morbrecia, dangling the bracelet from a spidery leg. She wasn't silly. "Undo the spell. Then you can have it."

The sorcerer was taken by surprise. He hadn't bargained for this. His plan had been to grab the charm bracelet and squash Morbrecia flat! Finish her off. Squish, squish. Bye-bye. She was nothing but trouble anyway.

Now he was afraid she might just scuttle off. Hide the precious bracelet somewhere out of reach. It was a tricky situation. He must take care! Zorgan squeezed a smile from his lips. Then he said sweetly:

"Trust me, Morbrecia. You know I only want to

help. I'll make you powerful. You'll be queen instead of Charm. Think of it! *Queen* Morbrecia!"

Morbrecia had to admit, it did sound good.

"Fairsay,"✱ she replied. "But fix this spell or else . . ."

Zorgan couldn't risk arguing. Quickly he chanted:

"*ADIN CHARA, CHARAN IDAR.*
*ARACH NIDA — VASHOOM!*"

✱ ✱ ✱ ✱ ✱ ✱ ✱ ✱ ✱ ✱ ✱ ✱ ✱ ✱ ✱ ✱ ✱ ✱ ✱ ✱ ✱ ✱ ✱ ✱

⭐ **Fairsay** – ok, all right

There was a blinding green flash as the spell broke, and Morbrecia was herself once more.

For a tantalizing few minutes, Morbrecia toyed with the bracelet. She turned it round and round, delighted by each charm: a lucky horseshoe, for a unicorn perhaps?; a coin for good fortune; a lantern to light the way; the daintiest snowflake . . . She couldn't wait to wear it! But she was greedy and ambitious too. If there was a chance Zorgan could work his magic . . . If he could *really* make the bracelet super-powerful . . .

"Enough!" cried Zorgan, suddenly snatching the bracelet. "Foolish girl! If you thought for a moment I'd let you have it, you are very much mistaken."

And he put it on. One of the charms was a heart with a little lock. Another was a tiny key. Together they fastened the bracelet securely round his wrist. Zorgan stretched out his wrist and, for a fleeting moment, there was a look of ecstasy on his face. Each silver charm glistened so brightly! Strange. He had expected the bracelet to feel cool. But no! It was warm, and getting warmer. Then it turned HOT! Scorching, burning, blazing hot. The charms shimmered with heat.

"Owwwwwwooooooooo!" howled Zorgan.

Morbrecia stood transfixed by this turn of events. She was fascinated! Perhaps, she thought, the bracelet recognised her as its rightful owner? Was it teaching Zorgan a lesson for tricking her? Yes! That was it! She stood and watched as Zorgan leaped around in agony, tearing at the burning band.

"Horrid, horrid thing! Get off!" he screamed, desperate to be rid of it. He clawed at the clasp, yelling as it burnt his fingers, until *SNAP!* The clasp broke and Zorgan wrenched the bracelet off.

Morbrecia was convinced the bracelet wouldn't burn her. It was rightfully hers! Surely it would cool as soon as SHE touched it? Seizing her chance, she lunged forward. But she was too late.

As Zorgan wrenched the bracelet apart, he flung it with *such* force that twelve of the thirteen charms broke off. They flew far and wide, all over Karisma. But the heart clung to the bracelet. They remained together.

## Six

"**W**hoop-whoop!" cried Fig.
It was some time since Sesame
and the tunganora had left Dork and his
men, searching for the bracelet. Sesame
had been walking along, deep in thought.
First there were the gribblers the gatekeeper
had warned her about. What *were* they? Where
did they hang out? Then, and much more
intriguing, was this news about a spider stealing
a bracelet! And who was Queen Charm? Sesame
was now convinced that she had been sent to
Karisma to find the missing bracelet . . .

*Whoop-whoop!*

The cry suddenly jolted Sesame back to the
present. She'd almost forgotten about Fig!

The tunganora was tugging at her arm and
pointing to some blue leaves, growing at
the top of a tall tree.

"Hungry?" said Sesame, stopping
to comfort him.

45

Fig responded by sucking his paws noisily.

"R-i-g-h-t," she said, looking up between the branches. "So, you want *those* leaves and you'd like me to get them?"

*Whoop!* They understood each other perfectly! It was a bit scary but eventually Sesame managed to climb to the top and bring down a handful of leaves. After hastily eating them all, Fig gave a joyful *whoop!* and turned a somersault. Sesame laughed.

"Come on," she said cheerfully, "your mum can't be far away." She hoped she was right.

Shortly afterwards, they came to a clearing where a lot of trees had been cut down. There were fallen tree trunks and twisted branches everywhere! Sesame didn't think the map would be much use here, so she put it away in her pocket. She led Fig through the tangled undergrowth, stepping over logs and ducking under boughs. They were making slow but steady progress, until they tripped on some sticks . . . *SNAP! CRACK!*

"Whoooaaaaar!" yelled Sesame.

"*Whooooo!*" cried Fig.

They had fallen into a pit. Luckily their fall was broken by something soft and hairy. Something PINK and hairy.

"Moomoo!"✱ cried Fig, joyfully. He had found his mother.

Recovering from her fall, Sesame stood up and introduced herself to Fig's mother. At first the tunganora was nervous, but eventually Sesame discovered that her name was Hob.

And now that Fig and Hob had been happily reunited, she set about getting everyone out of the pit.

Although the pit wasn't very deep, Sesame could see there was no way a tunganora could escape from it on its own. This was obviously a trap! Sesame was worried that whoever made it might return at any minute and find them.

Sesame crouched down.

"Quick!" she said to Hob, "stand on me. I'll pass Fig up when you're out."

* * * * * * * * * * * *

✱　**Moomoo** — mother

Fortunately it didn't take long for Hob to realise that Sesame was trying to help. So she jumped on Sesame's shoulders and climbed out easily. Then, when Fig had been rescued, Hob reached down and hoisted Sesame to the top.

"Who do you think did this?" asked Sesame, clambering over the edge.

"Gribblers!" replied Hob, speaking at last. She spat the word out in disgust.

"Mmm!" said Sesame. "I've heard about them. Who are they?"

"Vile creatures!" said Hob. "Sharp teeth. Bad breath!"

"And the trap?" queried Sesame.

"To catch us . . ." Hob said.

But she was careful not to frighten Fig by saying what would have happened, if they had.

"They want our trees," she explained. "It's the leaves, you see? They'll do anything for the leaves." Hob picked up a few wilted ones that had been left lying on the ground.

"To eat?" asked Sesame.

"No!" said Hob. "They make potions. They think it makes them strong."

At the sight and mention of his favourite food, Fig started up an insistent *Whoop-whoop-whooping* wail. He was obviously still hungry. So, after thanking Sesame for her help, Hob and Fig went off in search of fresh leaves.

As Sesame watched them go, she thought the plight of the tunganora sounded familiar. Their trees were being cut down by greedy gribblers. Their food and habitat was being destroyed. Something she'd heard or read maybe? But she couldn't quite remember now.

Sesame looked at her watch. The troll had warned her to be back at the gate by sunset, and she didn't want to be late. But wow! Something strange had happened. The dial on her watch had changed. Instead of numbers, there were pictures of the sun, moon and stars.

"What's going on?" said Sesame.

At first she hadn't a clue how to tell the time with it. Then she noticed the sun was slowly going down.

"Oh, I get it," she said. "When the sun goes behind the hill . . . it's sunset. Funky!"

She reckoned she had about an hour left to explore, before it was time to go.

# Seven

"AAAAARH!" screamed Morbrecia, as the bracelet and charms scattered in all directions. Her dark eyes flashed with fury.

"That was mine!" she yelled at Zorgan. "Mine, you MAGWORT!"★

Zorgan winced. He rubbed the place on his wrist where the charms had burned. Besides, he hated being called a magwort. That really hurt.

"Out!" he cried. "Get out!"

"I'm going!" said Morbrecia. "But I'll get those charms back! Then you'll be sorry. I'll find them and DESTROY you!"

"On the contrary," said Zorgan. His tone was quiet but chilling. "You're the one who'll be sorry, Morbrecia. I'll make very sure of THAT!"

Morbrecia raced from Zorgan's tower. As she ran through shrouds of early morning mist, her black robes flapped like bats' wings. She was heading for the Dark Forest, to meet up with the gribblers. She'd get them to help her.

* * * * * * * * * * * * * * * * * * * * * * * * * *

★ **Magwort** – probably the worst name you could call anyone! General term for a fool

51

Even as she took a shortcut past Queen Charm's palace, she was still spitting with rage at Zorgan's trickery. And the sight of her sister's palace did nothing to improve her temper.

"I went to all that trouble to steal the bracelet," Morbrecia hissed through clenched teeth, "and that slitey* sorcerer throws it away!"

Entering the forest, Morbrecia came to a curtain of creepers. The writhing tentacles caught in her hair and she had to wrestle her way through.

* * * * * * * * * * * * * * * * * * * * * * * * * * * *

⭐ **Slitey** – sly or untrustworthy

"Balam★ weeds!" she cursed them.
"Out of my way!"

It was eerily still among the trees, broken only by the sudden *swish!* of dry leaves, as an animal scuttled to hide. It was as if the forest was holding its breath in fear.

Morbrecia was hurrying along a twisty path, when Officer Dork and his search party appeared. They were returning to the palace after an unsuccessful morning. Dork was dreading telling Queen Charm they hadn't found the bracelet. But when he saw Morbrecia, he brightened up. Meeting her, by chance, had made his day.

"Princess Morbrecia," he said bowing low. "How mice to feet you!"

The words came out all wrong and he blushed bright red. To make matters worse, his men had begun to snigger.

"What?" snapped Morbrecia. She'd never liked Dork. She thought he was a creep.

He began again.

"I s-s-said how m-m-mice to . . ."

An awkward silence followed before Dork tried once more. He'd thought of a piece of news that might interest her.

* * * * * * * * * * * * * * * * * * * * * * * * *
★ **Balam** – cursed, an angry exclamation

53

"We've been searching for the queen's bracelet," he said. "It was stolen last night."

"Really," said Morbrecia flatly.

It wasn't *quite* the response he'd expected. So he leaned closer and added, "By a SPIDER!"

Dork had high hopes this last detail might result in Morbrecia squealing with fright. But it didn't work out that way. Morbrecia's eyes positively glowed with excitement.

"Did it scare her?" she asked.

"Queen Charm was frightened out of her royal wits," replied Dork.

"Vixee!" exclaimed Morbrecia, gleefully.

And an idea suddenly struck her. Dork might be a creep but he could be a useful one. She smiled at him.

"If you find the bracelet or . . ." she hesitated. She must be careful not to say too much. If she revealed that the charms had been scattered – he'd be suspicious.

He'd want to know how she knew. So she finished in a vague sort of way. ". . . you know, find anything. You'll tell me won't you? We must all do our best to find the bracelet and return it to . . . its rightful owner, mustn't we?"

How cleverly Morbrecia concealed her true intentions! And Dork didn't suspect a thing. He bowed again and said:

"Of course! Anything for you, Princess Morbrecia."

It suddenly occurred to him to mention his meeting with Sesame Brown, earlier that morning. He slightly altered the facts, to make it sound as if he'd ordered the Outworlder to search for the bracelet. Dork thought Morbrecia would be impressed. Instead she was furious.

"Blatz!" ✱ she exclaimed. "You can't trust an Outworlder! What if this Sesame Brown finds the bracelet? Supposing she keeps it? What then? Keep looking, Dork!" she ordered. "We've got to find the bracelet before SHE does!"

And with that, Morbrecia stormed off to meet the gribblers.

* * * * * * * * * * * * * * * * * * * * *

✱ **Blatz** – a really angry exclamation

# Eight

A hedge towered above her. Sesame had left the Dark Forest and arrived in front of an enormous wall of green. From somewhere high above came the sound of hedge clippers.

*Snip-snip. Snip-snip. Snip-snip!*

Sesame craned her neck to look up. At the top, she saw two gardeners clipping the topiary. From where Sesame was standing they looked tiny. One gardener was clipping a cat, with a long curled tail. The other was shaping a dolphin.

When they caught sight of Sesame, they looked very surprised. But they seemed friendly.

"Helloo!" called one.

"Fairday!"* said the other, waving his shears.

"Hi!" said Sesame. She was curious about the topiaries. "What are they?" she asked.

"Each represents a charm on the queen's bracelet," said the first gardener, who was now skilfully trimming the cat's tail.

"I see," said Sesame. "How many are there?"

"Thirteen!" shouted the second, giving the dolphin one last *snip!*

Sesame looked along the top of the hedge. From where she was standing she could see a crescent moon, star, seashell, horseshoe and a butterfly. There were others but they were too far away to see clearly.

"Can I see them all?" asked Sesame, eager to find out more about the bracelet.

And the gardeners, who were only too pleased to show off their work, allowed Sesame into the palace gardens. She found a gap in the hedge, by a ladder, just wide enough for her to squeeze through.

* * * * * * * * * * * * * *

★ Fairday – a typical Karisman friendly greeting

57

On the other side the gardens seemed to go on for ever. The palace looked very grand, with a lake and fountain playing, nearby. There were colourful flowers everywhere, and some statues too.

"Wow!" exclaimed Sesame.

It all looked so amazing. She set off along a path, past some strange-looking plants. Over there was a pumpkin patch with the funkiest fruits Sesame had ever seen. A purple pumpkin was popping seeds.

"Cool!" she cried, nimbly catching a pumpkin seed in mid-flight. It tasted good, so she caught and nibbled some more as she wandered along. In a while, the path divided.

"Which way now? Left or right?" she said aloud.

She decided right and, almost immediately, came to the entrance of a maze. It was as if something had guided her there, and was telling her to go inside! But she thought to check her watch before she went in.

By this time the sun had reached the top of the hill. Sesame calculated, as best she could, there was about half an hour to sunset. I'll be quick, she thought. I'm good at mazes. And who knows what I might find!

The paths went round in circles. First Sesame walked down a long path and turned left. Then left again. Now right. On and on and round and round – this way and that – until at last . . .

"Yesssss!" Sesame congratulated herself proudly. She had found the heart of the maze. It was the smallest circle of all and in the middle was a large pot, planted with flowers. Sesame thought they looked like poppies. And for a reason she couldn't think of, they reminded her of someone . . .

Sesame stopped daydreaming and snatched another look at her watch. True, she'd found the middle pretty quickly, but she still had to find her way out. Now she'd have to hurry. She was about to leave when something shiny caught her eye. A silvery object was caught up in the poppies. Carefully, she pulled the flowers apart and reached in . . .

It was the missing bracelet!

"Oh!" she gasped. It was beautiful. But there was only one charm on it – a tiny heart with a lock. She turned the bracelet around and counted twelve more rings where the other charms should have been. What a shame! thought Sesame. Perhaps they've fallen in here?

She peered into the poppies again. No, nothing there.

"Right," she said. "One bracelet. One charm. It's a start. Now for the other twelve!"

Sesame was determined to find all the charms for the queen. In fact, she would make it her mission to succeed! She'd be a . . . *Charmseeker*. Yes! That was it. She said it aloud:

"Charmseeker!"

And it sounded just right.

Sesame put the bracelet in her pocket – the one where she'd put her map – but now she discovered it wasn't there. "Oh no!" she cried. "I must have dropped it somewhere." But there was no time to worry about that now. She must find her way out of the maze and get to the gate before it closed.

*Can you find the path Sesame took to get to the centre of the maze and out again?*

# Nine

An order had been issued from the palace to the twelve gatekeepers of Karisma. It read:

> **Stolen!**
> The bracelet belonging to Her Majesty Queen Charm was stolen last night from the palace. The identity of the intruder is unknown, but it is believed to be a large spider. Gatekeepers are ordered to report any spider seen acting suspiciously.
> It is of the utmost importance that the bracelet and its thirteen charms are returned to Her Majesty.
> By Order. *Palace Secretary*

At dawn the Silversmith had been to the palace, to warn the queen of her fears.

"Zorgan's behind this," she began angrily. "I just know it!" She tossed her long, silvery hair to one side. "There's so much at stake. If he has the bracelet, well . . . I dread to think of the consequences!"

Charm was only too well aware. She felt angry and upset that this could have happened, here at the palace, surrounded by all her guards!

"I did my best to protect it!" she said.

"I know," said the Silversmith, gently. "You're not to blame. No one could have done more to keep it safe. But even you are powerless against the forces of evil that were here last night!"

The Silversmith frowned. How could she tell Charm that she had a nagging feeling her sister was involved somehow? The ugly thought had been buzzing round her head like a fly, ever since she had awoken last night, convinced that the bracelet had been stolen. And it had. But she had no proof about Morbrecia. Was that just intuition?

She decided, for the time being, to keep these thoughts to herself and quickly changed the subject. She had some good news.

"I've found someone who can help," she said.

"Who?" asked Charm.

"Sesame Brown," said the Silversmith. "A Charmseeker. She arrived this morning."

The queen was intrigued. She'd never heard of a Charmseeker before, let alone met one.

"I should like to meet Sesame Brown," she said. "Please, invite her to the palace."

"I can't do that," said the Silversmith. She must choose her words carefully. Losing the charm bracelet was bad enough. But she also knew the charms had been scattered. For, at the very moment Zorgan had so ruthlessly cast the charms away, the Silversmith had felt a wrenching pain. "I'm afraid you can't see her until the bracelet . . . the charms . . . everything's been found."

"Why?" said Charm, sounding disappointed. Then she added, wryly. "After all, I am the Queen! Surely you can grant me that wish?"

"Your Majesty," replied the Silversmith firmly, "Sesame must be left to work in her own way. In her own time. She has a special gift, you see? The gift to *seek*."

The queen didn't really understand but she knew it was no good arguing with the Silversmith. She had her own way of doing things. Besides, she trusted her completely.

"Then I'll just have to be patient, won't I," she said with a sigh. "But it all sounds very mysterious!"

When the Silversmith returned home, she lit thirteen candles and named them after the charms.

They were magic candles – each one would burn until its charm had been found – however long it took.

The gribblers were furious! Three of them were standing around the empty pit, dribbling and cursing. The biggest of them, Varg, bared his teeth. They were a disgusting shade of yellow and some were missing altogether.

"Shumone's been meshing wiv our shtuff," he said, showering the others with a spray of slime. "You can shmell 'em!"

"Yeah!" said another, called Gorz. He sniffed noisily.

"Poooeee!" exclaimed the youngest one, Bod.

It was remarkable the gribblers could smell anything apart from their own awful stench. Their breath smelled like rotting fish – only ten times worse. Varg spoke again.

"I knows we had one," he growled. Heard it go down. Should've shorted it meshelf. Bet it were a biggun!"

Varg was, of course, talking about Hob. It made him mad as a maggot to think that someone had released a tunganora from the trap. Just when they were doing their best to get rid of them! Those wretched pink creatures lived off the leaves they wanted, to make potions.

He spat out a dollop of slime that whizzed down into the pit. It landed on something at the bottom with a resounding *SPLAT!*

"What's that?" said Gorz, peering over the side. He had sharp, piggy eyes. "There's something down there. Look!"

Bod jumped into the pit, then scrambled out again, clutching something in his hand. It was Sesame's map!

"Give it here!" said Varg, snatching the map and cuffing Bod round the ear, because he felt like it.

At that precise moment Morbrecia arrived. The

gribblers shuffled awkwardly as she approached.

"What's that?" she demanded.

Varg handed her the map. Morbrecia scowled when she read what the gatekeeper had written:

## Outworlder - Tourist

"So!" she snarled. "Sesame Brown has been here! She's a meddler, make no mistake!"

She still couldn't believe how stupid Dork had been, for telling this stranger about the bracelet!

As soon as Gorz heard the word Outworlder, he held his nose.

"I knew it!" he cried. "Dats wot de smell woz. It's right up by dose!" Then he sneezed.

## A-H-H-H-TISHOOOO!

It was not a pretty sight.

Varg scowled.

"Shees been meshing in our bishness!" he explained to Morbrecia, who had ducked to avoid the spit. "I'll shkewer her shkull!" he hissed.

"I'll boil her brains!" said Gorz.

"I'll have her eyeballs for lollipops!" said Bod.

A cold smile escaped from Morbrecia's lips. She could always rely on the gribblers to cheer her up.

"Good!" she said. "Sniff her out. Let's be rid of her! And there's something else. I need your help to find a bracelet . . ."

## Ten

Sesame came out of the maze and ran to the hedge. She was starting to panic. The sun was going down fast and soon it would be sunset. What if she got to the gate too late? What if it was closed? What if . . . ?

"Oh stop what iffing!" she told herself crossly. "THINK!"

Where was the gap? She quickly looked along the bottom of the hedge, from side to side. But it was like a solid wall – not a gap or gate to be seen!

She tried to remember the spot where she'd seen the two gardeners working on some topiary.

The gap was near there. One had been clipping a . . . what was it? Then she remembered. A cat! "Easy peasey," she said. "Find the cat and I'm out."

Sesame expected to spot it straightaway but she didn't. Instead she found herself near where she'd first spotted the other topiaries – but then they'd been too far away to see clearly. Close up, she could now see these were a heart, a key, a cloverleaf, a snowflake and a lantern. And what was that round one? A coin? Sesame remembered that each neatly clipped shape represented one of the thirteen charms.

But where was the cat?

Sesame looked carefully around the enormous hedge. And there, quite a long way off, she could just make out a dolphin and . . . the CAT! She ran as fast as she could until she found the gap. Then she scrambled through, back into the Dark Forest.

It looked different somehow. The setting sun cast a pinkish glow over everything. Sesame wished she still had the map! She had just started to walk, when Hob appeared. She'd been waiting to show Sesame the way.

"One good turn deserves another," she told Sesame. "Quick! Come with me. The gribblers are out to get you!"

This alarming piece of news took Sesame completely by surprise.

"How do they know about me?" she asked.

As they hurried through the forest Hob explained how this unfortunate situation had come about. She told Sesame she had overheard three gribblers talking.

"They found your map," said Hob. "You dropped it down the pit."

"Ah!" said Sesame. "So that's where it went."

"Morbrecia's got it now," said Hob. She was lolloping along at a steady pace and Sesame was doing her best to keep up. She could feel the bracelet jiggling about in her pocket and she didn't want to lose it.

"Who's Morbrecia?" she asked, a bit out of breath.

"Queen Charm's sister," said Hob. "Princess Morbrecia. Mixes with the likes of Zorgan and the gribblers. Bit of a witch, if you ask me."

Sesame was confused. Who was Zorgan? And why was Morbrecia like a witch? She was about to ask, when Hob stopped dead in her tracks. She sniffed.

"Fish," she whispered.

"In a forest!" said Sesame.

Then she got wind of it too. A disgusting smell of rotting fish filled the air.

"Ugh!" she said, holding her nose.

"Sssh!" said Hob. "Gribbler!"

In the dim light of the forest, against an ever reddening sky, Sesame saw a hideous creature. It was Varg and he was heading slowly their way. Sesame wanted to scream. She cupped her hands over her mouth, her stomach churning like a blender.

Varg's hooded eyes had picked out two shadowy shapes among the trees. Hob could have told Sesame a useful thing or two about gribblers. She knew that their sense of smell and hearing remained good at all times. But at dusk their eyesight is poor. Their hooded eyes can't adjust to the change of light. But this was no time for a lecture on gribblers. Instead she whispered urgently:

"Look! There's the gate."

Sesame looked. She reckoned the gate was about twenty paces away. And she saw the troll preparing to lock it. It was nearly sunset! Hob kept her eyes on Varg.

"I'll deal with *him*," she said "Now run for it. Fast as you can. GO!"

And Sesame ran.

Had she looked back she would have seen Hob crashing through the undergrowth, dangerously near the gribbler.

Sesame raced on, her heart pounding. The troll had put the key in the lock and was about to turn it.

"Wait!" cried Sesame. "Oh, please WAIT!"

"You're late!" said the troll. He stood, arms folded, foot tapping. He pointed to a notice from the palace and Sesame read it:

> **Stolen!**
> The bracelet belonging to Her Majesty Queen Charm was stolen last night from the palace. The identity of the intruder is unknown, but it is believed to be a large spider. Gatekeepers are ordered to report any spider seen acting suspiciously.
> It is of the utmost importance that the bracelet and its thirteen charms are returned to Her Majesty.
> By Order. *Palace Secretary*

Sesame was very afraid the troll wouldn't let her through if he knew she had the bracelet – and there wasn't time to explain about her mission now!

So she said nothing and he opened the gate.

"Next time, don't be LATE!" he said.

And 'late' was the very last word Sesame heard, as she fell, fell, fell into a silvery mist . . .

72

# Eleven

"L ATE! . . . late!"

"What?" said Sesame, her head in a spin.

"I said, I'm sorry I'm *late*!" Maddy was saying. "I tried to get here on time. Honestly, Sessy. But I forgot my purse and had to . . ."

"Yeah. Fine, fine," said Sesame.

She was bemused to find herself back outside **Tip Tops** on the High Street. She glanced at her watch. The sun, moon and stars had gone. Her watch was back to normal. It was just five past ten. Maddy thought Sesame was checking to see how late she was.

"I know you're cross," she said. "But I did try!"

"No. I'm not," said Sesame.

And she flung her arms round Maddy and hugged her.

"Oh, Maddy, I'm SO pleased you're here," she said. "I've got so much to tell you!"

"R-i-g-h-t . . ." said Maddy, wondering what was coming next. Sesame looked as if she was going to

73

burst. "You haven't got a crush on a *boy* or something?"

"No way!" said Sesame, pulling a face. "Something . . . more exciting. But it'll have to wait."

"Oh, that's not fair!" complained Maddy. "We never have secrets. We tell each other everything!"

Sesame knew she *would* tell Maddy sometime. But not now. She'd find the right moment to tell her friend about an extraordinary place called Karisma. That's if it DID exist!

"I will, I *promise*," said Sesame. "Look," she said, quickly changing the subject and pointing to the window. "I've just seen this fabulous top . . ."

Sesame stopped. She couldn't believe her eyes. The top with the silvery heart wasn't there.

"Which one?" asked Maddy.

"Er . . . it's gone," said Sesame, flatly.

Her head still felt a bit funny. Had she imagined everything? She was so sure it had all started here. Maddy rolled her eyes.

"You're acting weird today!" she said, slipping her arm through Sesame's. "Come on. Let's go in."

When Sesame got home that afternoon, she raced upstairs to her room. She took the bracelet, with its one remaining charm, out of her pocket, to look at it.

"Oh dear!" she sighed, cradling the tiny heart in her hand. She was more determined than ever to go back to Karisma, to look for the other charms. "I haven't a clue how to get back there," she confided in her teddy, Alfie. "But I'm a Charmseeker, see? I'll find a way!"

Until then, Sesame would have to keep the bracelet safe and she knew just the place. The jewellery box, beside her bed! She knew it had a tray, which was divided into thirteen little sections, with a larger one in the middle.

"Perfect!" she said, carefully placing the bracelet and the heart inside the box. She felt strangely excited, seeing them there. Her mission had just begun!

"One day, I'll return the bracelet to Queen Charm with ALL thirteen charms," she told Alfie.

And she closed the lid.

Sesame looked again at the picture painted on it. She now saw that the circle in the picture was a bracelet – EXACTLY like the one she'd found in Karisma. And those thirteen symbols? Sesame was sure it was a code.

"I'm going to crack it or bust!" she said. And went to find a pencil and paper.

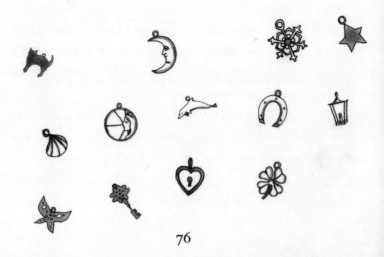

**Can you crack the code before Sesame?**
**Each symbol represents a letter.**

*CLUE: First, work around the outer circle of symbols to solve the puzzle.*

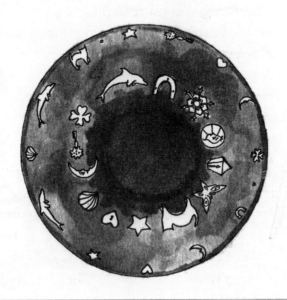

_____

_____

_____

* * * * * * * * * * * * * * * * * * * * * * * * * * *

**Jewellery box code:** A – heart  B – horseshoe  C – star
D – crown  E – dolphin  F – pumpkin  G – fairy  H – key
I – candle  J – coin  K– unicorn  L – shell  M – clover
N – mermaid  O – butterfly  P – gate  Q – sun  R – moon
S – troll  T – cat  U – witch  V – tree  W – snowflake
X – dragon  Y – lantern  Z – flower (poppy)

Later, Sesame was in the kitchen with her gran. Lossy was busy preparing supper and Sesame had fed Chips and Pins. The kittens had just settled down to the serious business of washing and Sesame sat watching them, deep in thought.

"Pass the butter," said Lossy, vigorously mashing a pot of potatoes. When Sesame didn't respond, she looked up. Her granddaughter was miles away!

"Hell-lo. Anyone there?" said Lossy, waving.

Sesame laughed.

"Sorry. What did you say?"

"Everything all right?" said Lossy, reaching for the butter. She knew Sesame's moods so well. Ever since her mother had died, Lossy had helped to bring her up. They were very close.

"Mmm," said Sesame.

"Mmm what?" said Lossy, scooping creamy potatoes into a bowl. There was *something* on Sesame's mind, she was sure.

"G-r-a-n," began Sesame slowly. "Do you believe in . . . do you think there are . . . other worlds?"

"Phew!" said Lossy. "Now there's a question. You been reading those spacey sci-fi books?"

"No," said Sesame. "I mean *real* worlds with real people and . . . things."

Lossy gave this some careful thought. Sesame was so like Poppy, always questioning and wanting to find out more.

"Well, I don't see why not," she said.

And for the time being that was that. There were a million things Sesame wanted to tell Lossy. But she couldn't. Not yet. Not until she'd worked out what had really happened.

It had all begun with that top in the window. She was so *sure* it had been there. And, if it hadn't been for the bracelet, she would have thought she'd imagined it all.

But the bracelet WAS here, in her jewellery box. As real, as real as could be!

After supper Lossy switched on the television to watch the news. Chips and Pins were asleep and Sesame realised she was sleepy too.

"What time will Dad be home?" she said, yawning.

"Late," said Lossy. "He's at that football match, remember?"

Sesame was about to say goodnight, when she caught snippets of a news item on the TV. The newscaster was saying something about . . . *our*

79

She was keen to know what it was all about, so she waited to see. Apparently, a special organisation had been set up to rescue homeless apes. The rainforest, where they lived, was being cleared for palm oil crops. The apes had nowhere to live and were starving.

"I read about that this morning," said Sesame.

Then some pictures of orphan orangutans appeared on the screen.

"Poor little mites!" said Lossy. "Thank goodness someone's taking care of them."

"Yes," said Sesame. "I wish I could too!"

And suddenly a vision of Hob and Fig flashed through her head. What had happened to Hob? She said she would deal with that gribb . . . Sesame couldn't bear to think about that awful creature and shut her eyes.

"Look at you," said Lossy, "you're half asleep. Now off to bed with you!"

So Sesame kissed her gran and went upstairs.

There was a bag from **TIP TOPS** under her pillow that she hadn't noticed earlier. Sesame read the note attached to it:

Dear Ses,
Forgot to give this to you this morning.
Hope you like it.
Love,
Dad xx

Inside was the bright red top with the sparkly heart. And when Sesame picked it up, a sprinkling of silver dust fell to the floor . . .

# Twelve

The Silversmith sighs. The first of the thirteen candles flickers and goes out. Twelve candles remain lit. It's a start. The bracelet has been found with the heart clinging to it. Sesame's quest has begun!

The Silversmith knows Sesame will return to Karisma. When she does, she will learn about the magic of the charms and how important it is to find them all. She has the gift to seek and she must continue her search.

Already there are signs that Karisma is changing, because without the bracelet, the balance of nature is awry. And everyone has been talking about the change in the weather! How, without warning, the gentle summer rains have suddenly turned into torrents; how the crops, ready for harvest, have been ruined by floods.

And only today she's noticed the silver pool – it's lower than she's ever known! What will happen if it dries up? What if there is no more silver? But that's another story! It must keep for another day.

the
Silver
Pool

For my parents –
Douglas and Georgina
With love and gratitude
Amy

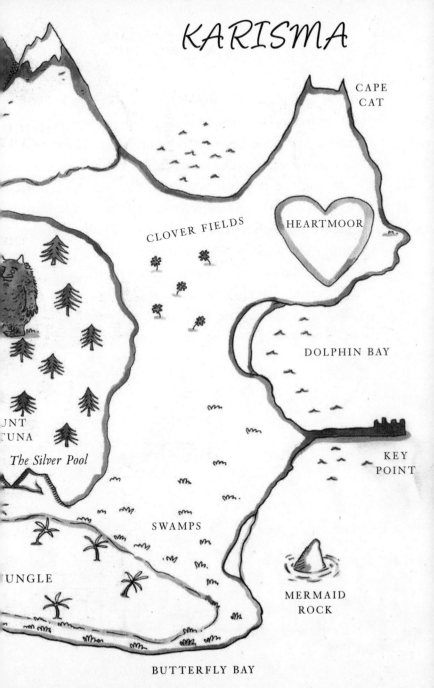

In the soft glow of candlelight the Silversmith sits and reflects. Her Charmseeker's quest has begun. Sesame has found the bracelet and heart charm, and has taken them to the Outworld for safekeeping.

One of the thirteen magic candles has gone out. Twelve lighted candles remain and each will burn until its charm has been found. Will Sesame find the courage to see her mission through?

"I have chosen well," says the Silversmith, confident she has made the right decision about Sesame Brown. "She will return to continue her quest, of that I have no doubt!"

# One

Zorgan paced
the floor, his
thoughts swirling
like a whirlpool,
as he dwelt on
some recent,
unfortunate
events. His plan to
take possession of
the bracelet had gone
badly wrong – his
old adversary the
Silversmith had seen
to that! At the
very thought of
her, fury welled up
inside him. He was
convinced she had
put a spell on the
bracelet to prevent
him, or anyone
but Queen
Charm,

from wearing it – the black mark on his wrist was a constant and painful reminder that it had done its job.

The sorcerer recalled the fleeting sensation of joy he'd experienced when he'd put the bracelet on. Oh! The power that should have been his! But no, it was not to be. Angrily, Zorgan banged his fist on a table, cursing himself for scattering the charms. Now he must find and destroy them. The race was on to get them back!

The *bang* startled three companions who were with Zorgan in his study. The bandrall, Vanda, perched on a high-backed chair and the pixie puppets, Nix and Dina.

"Two new creations of my own," Zorgan had told Vanda, when introducing the pixies for the first time. To the casual observer Nix and Dina looked like normal pixie girls, with their flowing hair and impish faces. But closer inspection would reveal cold crystal eyes and steely wings, fine as cobweb; the pixies could fly like deadly arrows and were programmed to obey Zorgan without question.

The sudden noise unsettled Vanda.

"Rashee, rashee," * cooed Zorgan soothingly,

* * * * * * * * * * * * * * * * * * * * * * * * * *

*Rashee – hush; be still; a word of reassurance

92

stroking her neck. Ever since Vanda had come to roost on Zorgan's Tower, he'd taken an instant liking to her. The two had become inseparable. She flapped her wings to steady herself, before settling again on the chair.

Vanda watched as Zorgan turned to Nix and Dina. They stood alert, awaiting orders.

"The time has come to try you out," said Zorgan. "Set you tasks. Test your skills."

Nix and Dina's sharp eyes glinted in anticipation.

"You remember that, er, unfortunate incident with the charm bracelet?" he said, admiring a large gaudy ring on his finger.

Zorgan paused, waiting to see if Nix and Dina understood. They responded immediately.

"Yes, Master!" they chorused.

"When you put the bracelet on, it burned you," said Nix.

"So you threw it away!" added Dina enthusiastically.

"Spallah!"* exclaimed Zorgan, delighted with their response. "Well, I must get those charms back and destroy them. But there are those who wish to keep them. They must be stopped!"

"Who?" asked Dina.

"Morbrecia, for a start," he replied. "Queen Charm's sister. She's determined to find them, foolish girl,

* * * * * * * * * * * * * * * * * * * * * * * * * * * *

*Spallah – excellent!; a triumphant expression

though I doubt they'll do her any good. Besides, she's mad at me!"

Dina remembered Zorgan had tricked Morbrecia into stealing the bracelet from the queen. She'd been furious when Zorgan threw it away.

"Orders understood!" said Dina, with a malicious grin.

"Good," said Zorgan.

"Who else?" asked Nix, eager to prove herself too.

Zorgan hesitated. He wasn't sure, but he'd heard stories about an Outworlder. A girl called Sesame . . . Sesame . . . *Brown*! She'd been seen near Charm's palace.

"There's a girl . . ." he said, his voice cold as ice. "An interfering Outworlder. She'll be sorry she ever set foot in Karisma. I want to know all about Sesame Brown!"

The pixies shuddered at the venom in his voice.

"It shall be done, Master!" said Nix and Dina.

And in a whirr of wings they were off.

Zorgan's study was circular, as were all the others in the tower, tiered like the layers of a cake. It was lined from floor to ceiling with bookshelves, perfectly curved to fit the walls. The sorcerer's library contained hundreds of books on Astronomy, Astrology, Folklore, Myth and Magic.

After Nix and Dina had gone, he crossed the room to select some books from the shelves. Vanda followed, alighting on a chandelier, the better to observe Zorgan from her lofty perch. She watched him now scanning a row of leather-bound volumes.

First Zorgan took down
A Discourse with Dragons

by Perdika Klum. The author, a famous dracomologist, had spent a lifetime studying dragons and had learned to speak their language – Dracodictum. There was a list of phrases in her book that he would find useful. Next he selected *A Pool of Silver* and, after a quick look along a row of encyclopedias, he found an old copy of *Rare Chants and Incantations*.

"Ah, yes," said Zorgan, blowing a layer of dust from the cover. "I'll need that too."

Clasping the weighty tomes to his chest, Zorgan staggered up the spiral staircase to his Star Room – exactly one hundred and ninety-five twisty steps to the top of the tower. Vanda flew ahead, screeching with delight, in her element to be flying higher and higher.

The Star Room was entirely encased in glass. Zorgan stood for a moment to catch his breath, and take in the view of the heavens. It was magnificent! The sheer vastness of the starry night sky never failed to enthral. Up here the sorcerer felt exhilarated. Here he could do magic!

Looking out across Karisma, Zorgan fixed his gaze on Mount Fortuna in the distance. In no time he had conjured a vision of the Silver Pool, and the Silversmith who had charge of it. He would soon have his revenge on her!

But to achieve that, he had work to do. Seating himself comfortably in an armchair, he opened *A Pool of Silver* and started to read . . .

# A Pool of Silver
## by the Silversmith

PUBLISHED BY FORTUNA BOOKS, KARISMA

## Introduction by the Silversmith

The liquid silver, found in a pool on Mount Fortuna, is unique to Karisma and quite unlike the precious metal of other worlds. The exact origin of the Silver Pool is unknown although one thing is certain; the pool has existed for as long as anyone can remember, because no matter how much silver is used the pool always refills itself — like magic!

Various stories have been told which attempt to explain how it may have come about but the most popular belief, held by Karismans today, is based on this intriguing legend.

# The Legend of the Silver Pool

*In far off days,* when dragons were as common as cats, a huge dragon called Agapogo* lived in a cave on Mount Fortuna, guarding a vast hoard of silver. A glittering pile of coins, candlesticks, dishes, plates, trays, jewellery and ornaments were piled high from floor to ceiling.

How Agapogo came by this amazing treasure or what she intended to do with it remains a mystery, but she defended the silver as if her life depended upon it. And, for a hundred years or more, no one dared come near. The sound of her roaring rumbled like thunder. People got so used to the noise, they took no notice. Until the day it stopped.

* * * * * * * * * * * * * * * * * * * * * * * * *

* **Agapogo** – a favourite name for dragons, means "to spit fire"

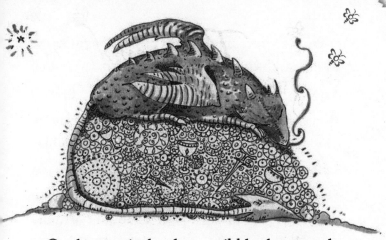

On that particular day a gribbler happened to be walking on the mountain and fell into the cave. When he recovered from his fall, the gribbler couldn't believe his luck. Here was a cave full of treasure and Agapogo sound asleep! He was sure he could steal some things and be off, before she woke up. Which might have worked, if the gribbler hadn't made a silly mistake. Because out of that enormous hoard he couldn't resist a fine silver goblet,* right under her nose!

* * * * * * * * * * * * * * * * * * * * * * * * *

*Goblet – a goblet, reputed to be the one stolen from Agapogo, is used by gribblers today in ceremonies, in which a powerful potion of leaves is sipped from the cup

Now a wiser thief might have thought twice about taking it, but not this one — it's well known that gribblers are not very bright. As soon as Agapogo felt the goblet move she opened her eyes and, seeing the gribbler standing there with her treasure, she got red-hot flaming mad! She swung her tail like a boolly* bat (a sure sign a dragon is really upset) sending everything flying. She roared SO loudly the mountain shook and flames burst from her nostrils like twin volcanoes.

And here is the most remarkable part of the story; the heat from those two blazing jets MELTED all the silver! Everything in that pile of treasure, down to the last tiny teaspoon,

* * * * * * * * * * * * * * * * * * * * * * * * *

*Boolly – a traditional Karisman ball game, played with a boolly bat and ball

dissolved like butter. It made a pool of silver
SO deep that Agapogo drowned.

How the gribbler survived Agapogo's flames
and lashing tail, we shall never know. But he
did and was the only one to witness the last
few moments of the dragon's life. The gribbler
is reputed to have told a friend:

"Agapogo tried to save herself, thrashing and
writhing about, something awful. Then she
gurgled and sank to the bottom and some big
bubbles came popping up."

A thin smile crept across Zorgan's lips as he closed the book.

"An unfortunate end for Agapogo," he told Vanda, at the same time reaching for *A Discourse with Dragons*. Then, having checked the pronunciation of some words in Dracodictum, Zorgan stood up and opened his copy of *Rare Chants and Incantations* at a page he had previously marked. Silently he mouthed the words. His hands shook. Zorgan was a powerful magician but he knew the risks. If he made a mistake, said one wrong word . . . there was no knowing what might happen! He took a deep breath and intoned:

★ APOST
    SNARGAL
        INCENDUS ★
            AGAPOGO!

A terrifying wind howled around the tower, and a blast of freezing air hit him full in the face. Then a ghostly dragon appeared, spinning out of nowhere like a tornado, its massive wings spread like sails. Silvery scales glowed eerily in the dark and in its scythe-like talons the phantom gripped a goblet. Zorgan had summoned the spirit of Agapogo – the dragon of the Silver Pool!

The force of the blast threw Zorgan to the floor. Vanda flew round the room in a panic, screeching in terror. Slowly picking himself up, Zorgan bowed and addressed Agapogo in Dracodictum:

> ★ "Drink the pool of silver dry, ★
> Or in its depths forever lie.
> ★ I command you to obey;
> Drain every drop without delay!"

A streak of lightning slashed the night sky, followed by an ear-splitting *crack* of thunder.

Then the spirit of Agapogo spoke, every word a blast of fury:

"You dare to call me from the deep
And wake me from eternal sleep?
Magician, you are a fool
To bid me drink the precious pool!
I'd fight this spell, if I were free,
Alas, this wicked plan must be.
It shall be done but you shall see,
Revenge shall be my guarantee!"

There was a blinding flash of light and a tremendous explosion. Instinctively Zorgan cowered and hid his face. When he looked again Agapogo's spirit had vanished in a cloud of smoke, leaving the sound of the spirit's words ringing in his ears.

# Two

It was a hot Friday afternoon, the last day of school before half-term. Sesame Brown sat in class, doodling in her notebook. Her best friend, Maddy Webb, was sitting next to her watching her doodle. Neither was concentrating much on what their history teacher, Mrs Wilks, was saying.

One reason was because Sesame and Maddy had just started riding lessons. Their riding instructor Miss Luck had suggested they come and help at the stables during half-term.

"You'll learn a lot about ponies that way," she'd said.

But there was another reason. Ever since her adventure in Karisma, Sesame kept thinking about what had happened there.

Mrs Wilks turned away to type something into her computer, and Maddy passed Sesame a note:

### What's that?

"Something I found," whispered Sesame. "When I went to . . ."

She stopped. Mrs Wilks had turned round and was looking straight at her!

"Who can tell me the name of the city?" she asked, pointing to an image she had just downloaded onto the white board. "Sesame. How about you?"

Sesame's class had been learning about the Romans, and Mrs Wilks had been telling them about a volcano, which had erupted and covered a city in hot ash.

Sesame panicked and out popped what she had been going to say to Maddy.

"Karisma!"

"No," said Mrs Wilks, giving Sesame a quizzical look. "I've never heard of *that* place. You must tell us about it sometime!"

The class giggled and Sesame wriggled in her seat.

"Anyone know the right answer?" said Mrs Wilks.

"Pompeii," said Olivia, who always paid attention.

Luckily for Sesame the bell went, and everyone hurried outside.

"Phew!" she said, as she and Maddy walked across the playground. "Supposing Mrs Wilks had made me talk about Karisma?"

"Well you've got to tell *me* about it," said Maddy. "You promised. Remember?"

It was true. Sesame had promised but, since then, she hadn't found the right time. And it couldn't be now because her gran, Lossy, and Mrs Webb were waiting to collect them from school.

"Tell you at sleepover tonight!" she said, giving Maddy their secret sign:

= True. I'll keep my word!

"Remember to bring your riding stuff for tomorrow," said Sesame. She knew how forgetful her friend could be.

"I will," said Maddy. "See you later!"

That evening, Maddy arrived at Sesame's house with a bulging bag. She had packed pyjamas, wash kit, food for a feast and all her riding gear. Unusually for Maddy, she hadn't forgotten a thing!

Mrs Webb and Sesame's dad chatted on the doorstep.

"Sorry, Nic," said Mrs Webb. "Looks like Maddy's come for a week not a night!"

Nic grinned.

"That's fine," he said, helping Maddy with her bag.

"They'll probably spend half the night gossiping," said Mrs Webb. "You know what they're like."

"I do!" said Nic. "Anyway, I'll drop them at the stables in the morning, on my way to work. That's if they're up in time."

"I heard that, Dad!" shouted Sesame, as she and Maddy struggled upstairs with the bag. "*We* will be ready way before *you*. So there!"

Their parents laughed.

"They probably will," said Nic. "Ready to ride at the crack of dawn!"

Sometimes Sesame and Maddy had sleepovers with their friends, Gemma and Liz. Those times were fun but tonight was extra special because it was just the two of them; actually four with the kittens, Chips and Pins, who'd crept up to Sesame's room to be with the girls. Sesame and Maddy loved spending time together. They would tell each other secrets they'd never tell anyone else. Although for Sesame there was her dad, and her gran Lossy. Ever since Sesame's mum had died, Lossy had been like a mother. But still, there were some things Sesame felt she couldn't talk about, even to her. Like going to Karisma! It was a secret she would share only with Maddy – for the time being.

Sesame picked up her teddy, Alfie, and held him tight.

"Remember that day I was waiting for you outside TIP TOPS?" she began.

"Mmm," said Maddy, chewing a sweet. "I was late, as usual!"

Maddy sat spellbound as Sesame told her how she had fallen into a strange world called Karisma. How she had met and helped two tunganoras* called Fig

* * * * * * * * * * * * * * * * * * * * * * * * * * * * *

*Tunganora – a small ape-like animal with long, pink shaggy hair, found only in Karisma. Their natural habitat is the Dark Forest, where they feed on the blue-spotted leaves of the tuntree

and Hob, who lived in the Dark Forest. How she had found a beautiful silver bracelet, with one heart charm, which belonged to Queen Charm. And finally, how Hob had helped her escape from a ghastly creature called a gribbler. By the end, Maddy's eyes and mouth were open wide in astonishment.

"Ses!" she whispered. "Did all that *really* happen? Honestly?"

"Yes," said Sesame. "Look."

She plonked Alfie on the pillow and picked up the jewellery box she always kept by her bed. First she showed Maddy the curious painting on the lid.

"Is it a code?" asked Maddy, examining the strange symbols.

"Yes," said Sesame, excitedly. "It took me ages but I cracked it. It spells 'CHARM BRACELET.'" Then she opened the box and revealed her biggest secret of all. There, on a tray, was Queen Charm's silver bracelet. And in a little section by itself, a heart charm with a tiny lock.

"Oh," gasped Maddy.

"The thing is, I've *got* to go back," said Sesame. "Twelve charms are still missing."

When Maddy looked more closely at the bracelet, she saw the empty rings where the other charms should be.

"I wonder what they are?" she said.

Sesame told her about the hedge she'd seen around Charm's palace gardens; it had shapes of all the charms clipped into it. She shut her eyes and tried to remember them.

"I saw a cat and a dolphin, a moon and star . . . a seashell, cloverleaf and . . . butterfly."

"That's seven," said Maddy, silently counting as Sesame spoke.

"Right," said Sesame, thinking hard. "I'm sure there was a horseshoe and a snowflake . . . a lantern and . . . a round one that could have been a coin. Oh, and a key!"

"That's twelve," said Maddy.

"And the heart makes thirteen!" said Sesame. "I've got to go back and find the missing ones. It's important Queen Charm has them back. Anyway, I want to know what happened to Hob. Supposing that gribbler . . ."

"How?" asked Maddy. "I mean, how will you get to Karisma?"

"That's the trouble," said Sesame. "I don't understand how I got there. So I haven't a clue how to get back!"

# Three

"**W**e're losing silver!" said the Silversmith. Her words echoed eerily around the cave.

– S–I–L–V–E–R . . . L–O–S–I–N–G . . . S–I–L–V–E–R!

"Hushish!"\*exclaimed the beautiful young woman standing next to her. It was Queen Charm. "First my charm bracelet and now this!"

It was alarming news to say the least. The Silver Pool of Mount Fortuna had always been full; no matter how much silver was used, the pool mysteriously refilled.

The two stooped to look more closely at the surface of the pool, shimmering way below.

"It's lower than when I last looked," said the Silversmith.

"Are you sure?" replied Charm, hoping against hope that she was mistaken.

"I'm certain of it," said the Silversmith. A frown wrinkled her delicate brow. "I noticed the change soon after your charm bracelet had been stolen. At

\* \* \* \* \* \* \* \* \* \* \* \* \* \* \* \* \* \* \* \* \* \* \* \* \* \*

\***Hushish** – a word used to express dismay

first I thought it was a coincidence but now . . . I'm not so sure. There may be a connection."

"What do you mean?" asked Charm, twisting a strand of fair hair round her finger. She was completely baffled; would she *ever* understand the Silversmith's quicksilver thoughts, flitting here and there, making pieces of the puzzle fall into place. "I seem to remember you thought Zorgan was involved?"

"Exactly!" said the Silversmith. "And something tells me he's behind this too—"

A sudden icy chill made her shiver and a ghastly vision flashed before her eyes. A dragon was writhing in the Silver Pool, fighting for its life! She gasped and shut her eyes. When she opened them again, the image had gone.

"What is it?" said Charm. "You look as if you've seen a ghost!"

"In a way . . . I think I have," said the Silversmith slowly. "Your Majesty, I believe Zorgan may have done something terrible."

"What?" said Charm.

"Well, he's probably furious because the charm bracelet won't work for him," said the Silversmith, her thoughts racing.

"Even if you're right," said Charm, "I still don't see how Zorgan can be blamed for this." She pointed to the pool.

The Silversmith hesitated before she replied. The full horror of what she was thinking made her head reel. When she spoke it was in a whisper.

"He may have put a spell on Agapogo to drain the pool. That . . . ghost I saw. It was—"

"Agapogo!" exclaimed Charm. "The dragon of the Silver Pool? But that's just a legend! A wonderful story, of course, and I loved reading it as a child but . . ."

She stopped. Something about the way the

Silversmith was looking at her made Charm realise she was perfectly serious.

"It *is* possible to summon the spirit of a dragon," said the Silversmith. "It's rarely done and no one but a magwort* would try it—"

There was a sharp intake of breath from Charm, as she took in the full meaning of what the Silversmith was saying. Instinctively, she went to clasp her charm bracelet for comfort. But of course it wasn't there.

"I feel so powerless without my bracelet," she told the Silversmith. "I need it now more than ever!"

Since her charm bracelet had been stolen, things had taken a turn for the worse. There had been a dramatic change in the weather – everyone was talking about it! Most of the summer crops had been ruined by heavy downpours of rain, which were unusual for

* * * * * * * * * * * * * * * * * * * * * * * * * * * * * *

**✱ Magwort** – Probably the worst name you could call anyone! General term for a fool

this time of year. The River Two Moons had burst its banks and flooded the surrounding fields. And, as if that wasn't bad enough, some skreel* had escaped from Morbrecia's lake; local farmers had reported seeing them, feeding off the carcasses of drowned animals. And now this loss of silver! It was a terrible state of affairs. She had to get her charm bracelet back and put things right.

The Silversmith read her thoughts; she'd been going to tell the queen some good news about the bracelet to cheer her up anyway.

"There's been a . . . development," she said, choosing her words carefully. "You remember I told you about the Charmseeker, Sesame Brown?"

"Yes," said Charm.

* * * * * * * * * * * * * * * * * * * * * * * * * * * *

*Skreel – small flesh-eating fish

"Well, she found your . . . *bracelet*," she said, emphasising the word.

"That's amazing!" exclaimed Charm. "Where is it?"

The Silversmith took a deep breath.

"Sesame has taken it to a safe place in the Outworld," she explained. "She found your bracelet with . . . just one charm. The heart. The other twelve charms are missing."

Charm felt giddy with emotion. She was elated to hear her bracelet had been found, but devastated about the charms that had been lost.

"Is Sesame coming back?" she asked. "Will she help us look for the missing charms?"

"Oh, yes," said the Silversmith, with a reassuring smile. "Sesame Brown will be back!"

# Four

Sesame and Maddy were up bright and early next morning, to go riding. They had finished their breakfast and washed up, long before Nic came into the kitchen.

"Come along, Dad," said Sesame, tapping her watch. "We don't want *you* to make us late!"

"Okay, okay, joke's on me!" said Nic, holding up his hands. "Be with you in five minutes."

He poured some coffee, grabbed a piece of toast and slung a camera over his shoulder. He worked as a photographer for *The Daily Times*. As Nic drove the girls to the stables, they chatted in the back of the car.

"I hope I ride Silver today," said Sesame. "He's my favourite."

"I like Muffin," said Maddy. "He's got a lovely soft nose."

"Sorry I can't stay to watch," said Nic. "I'm doing a charity fun run."

Sesame rolled her eyes.

"You're not actually *running*, Dad," she said, "just taking pictures."

"True," said Nic.

And they all laughed.

"It sounds cool anyway," said Maddy. "I'd like to be a photographer."

"I'm going to be a journalist like my mum," said Sesame. "We could be a news team, Maddy! I'd be an ace reporter, writing top stories. And you'd be taking all the pictures."

Miss Luck was busy organising riders and ponies for the first lesson. She had short, neatly cut hair and wore a smart riding jacket and jodhpurs.

"Hello!" she called to Sesame and Maddy, as they drove up. And because Nic hadn't met her before, he introduced himself.

"I'm Nic," he said. "Sesame's dad."

"Hi!" she said. "I'm Jodie. Jodie Luck."

They shook hands.

"Sorry I can't stay," said Nic, genuinely wishing he

could as he looked into Jodie Luck's soft blue eyes. "Work, you know," he muttered, feeling a bit embarrassed.

"Fine," said Jodie smiling. "Maybe another time? Sesame's doing really well."

"Yes," said Nic. "Definitely. Bye now, Ses. Bye, Maddy. Bye Miss . . ."

"Jodie," she said. "Call me Jodie."

Nic went off, leaving Jodie and the girls to walk across the yard.

"Please can I ride Silver today?" asked Sesame.

"Afraid not," said Jodie. "He's cast a shoe. The farrier is coming this morning. You can watch him shoe Silver if you like."

Sesame nodded enthusiastically.

"And me?" asked Maddy.

"Of course," said Jodie. "Now let's see which ponies you are riding."

There were six beginners in the lesson that morning. Sesame rode a chestnut pony called Fudge. Maddy was on Muffin. They walked, trotted and cantered round the indoor arena, while Jodie called out commands. Sesame and Maddy listened to every word she said.

At the end of the lesson, everyone untacked their ponies. Sesame and Maddy had just finished putting their saddles and bridles away, when Jodie popped her head round the tack-room door.

"Farrier's about to shoe Silver," she called.

They hurried across the yard to where the farrier's van was parked. It was like a forge on wheels. Inside were all the tools and things he needed. It even had a little furnace. Nearby an older girl was holding Silver. She was talking quietly to the pony, while he waited to be shod.

The farrier was busy heating a shoe in the furnace. He looked up when he saw Sesame and Maddy.

"Hello!" he said, taking the shoe out of the oven with a pair of pincers. It glowed red hot.

Sesame and Maddy looked horrified.

"Oh, poor Silver!" cried Sesame. "Won't that hurt?"

The farrier shook his head.

"Nope," he said, hammering the shoe into shape on the anvil. "This hoof's like your fingernails, see? Pony can't feel a thing."

"I hope he's right," whispered Maddy, half afraid to see what would happen.

She grabbed hold of Sesame and together they watched him place the hot shoe on Silver's foot. *Sssssssssh!* The horn sizzled and made a cloud of smoke. That was normal. But what happened next was not.

Sesame and Maddy stared at the smoke in a daze. They held each other tight as the cloud swirled around them. Only now it was more like a silvery mist. And, there in the middle, was a shiny horse-shoe, spinning round and round and round . . .

Sesame felt her feet leave the ground and was

aware that Maddy was still clinging to her, as they fell into the mist. There was a sudden rush of wind and then they were falling . . . spinning . . . turning head-over-heels until,

SLAP!
SPLASH!

Sesame and Maddy were up to their necks in water!

## Five

The magnificent runghorn,* Stanza, was the first to see them arrive. As one of the twelve gatekeepers of Karisma, he had been standing guard keeping a sharp look out for Sesame Brown – a Charmseeker from the Outworld.** Queen Charm had told all her gatekeepers to expect Sesame at any time.

Stanza quivered with curiosity. He had been expecting one Outworlder, not two! And which one was Sesame Brown? He went and stood by the riverbank, waiting to find out . . .

"What the—" spluttered Maddy, floundering about in the water and frantically looking for Sesame.

"Make for the bank!" shouted Sesame, doing her best to swim there herself. Sesame and Maddy were still dressed in their riding clothes, which made swimming difficult. Sesame was

* * * * * * * * * * * * * * * * * * * * * * * * * * * *

**\*Runghorn** – this remarkable beast has a magical horn, which can perform many useful functions

**\*\*Outworld** – the name Karismans call our world

making good progress, when she saw a small black fin slice through the water to her right.

"Watch out for skreel!" warned Stanza.

Maddy was dog-paddling nearby.

"What are—?" she began.

"Keep going!" said Sesame.

Eventually Sesame managed to crawl up a slippery bank; scrambling to her feet, she came face to face with Stanza. The shock of falling into the river was nothing compared to Sesame's overwhelming delight at being back in Karisma, where she was quite sure she was. There was a squelching sound as Maddy came clambering up the riverbank after her.

"Fairday!"* Stanza greeted them.
He pointed his curly horn, first at
Sesame and then at Maddy, and asked:

"Which one of you is Sesame Brown?"

* * * * * * * * * * * * * * * * * * * * * * * * * * * *

*Fairday – a typical Karisman friendly greeting

"Me!" said Sesame brightly, wringing water from her hair. "And this is my best friend, Maddy Webb."

"Are you *both* Charmseekers?" the gatekeeper enquired.

Sesame beamed at Maddy.

"Yes!" she said. "We've come to look for the missing charms."

Meanwhile Maddy stood there dripping wet and speechless. She couldn't believe her eyes. There was so much to take in, not least the fact she had suddenly and unexpectedly become a Charmseeker! Then Stanza introduced himself.

"I'm Stanza," he said. "Gatekeeper Two."

At last Maddy found her voice.

"Hi!" she said weakly.

"Sorry about the gate," said Stanza, casually waving a hoof at a nearby bush. "Not easy to find, I'm afraid."

Sesame and Maddy could make out a small wooden gate, overgrown with briars.

"No wonder we missed it," said Sesame.

"And we did get a bit wet . . ." said Maddy, water now streaming down her legs.

"Quisto!✱ Silly me," said Stanza. Straightaway he pointed his horn at the girls and they felt as though they were engulfed in a stream of warm air. In no time, their clothes were completely dry.

* * * * * * * * * * * * * * * * * * * * * * * * * *

✱ Quisto – an exclamation of surprise

"Thanks!" said Sesame and Maddy together.

Sesame had a quick look around at their surroundings; nothing looked familiar and much of the land had been flooded. Some fields were still underwater.

"Where are we?" she asked the gatekeeper.

"River Two Moons," replied Stanza. Then he pointed to a high craggy mountain nearby. "And that's Mount Fortuna where we have our famous Silver Pool!"

"What's that?" asked Sesame.

"Ah, you do not know the Legend of the Silver Pool?" said Stanza, wistfully.

"No," said Sesame and Maddy.

"Well," said Stanza, "I must tell you . . ."

Sesame was intrigued – always curious to find out about things – but she was keen to start looking for the charms. This was no time for a story! But Stanza had already begun and it would have been rude to leave, so the girls sat by the riverbank and listened.

Stanza told the story well, recounting every detail about Agapogo and her vast hoard of silver.

"Poor dragon!" cried Sesame, when Stanza had finished. She was upset at the thought of *any* creature being hurt.

"Horrible," agreed Maddy.

"True," said Stanza. "It was a terrible way for Agapogo to die. But her legacy is the Silver Pool we have today. It has magical properties. The Silversmith used silver from that very pool to make Queen Charm's bracelet and charms . . ."

"Charms!" said Sesame, suddenly jumping to her feet. She wanted to ask Stanza about the Silversmith but knew they had to get going.

"Come on, Maddy," she said. "Let's start at the palace gardens.'

"Where you found the bracelet and heart?" asked Maddy.

"Yes," said Sesame. "The other charms might be there too. I left in such a hurry last time, I may have missed them."

Saying goodbye to Stanza, Sesame and Maddy set off at last.

"Gate Two closes at moonrise," he called. "Setfair!"*

The girls were passing the bush where Stanza had shown them the gate, when they heard what sounded like the frantic fluttering of wings.

Maddy took a step nearer and looked. At first she couldn"t see anything, then – a sudden glint among the leaves. And she could have sworn she saw an eye, clear as crystal, staring at her. But when she looked again it had gone.

* * * * * * * * * * * * * * * * * * * * * * * * * * * *

*Setfair – goodbye and good luck

# Six

Nix and Dina had flown like the wind from Zorgan's Tower. Soon they separated – two heartless pixies, each on a mission for their master . . .

I'm Dina. My mission is to stop Morbrecia finding the charms. I will not fail. Ha! Soon she won't be going anywhere, you'll see!

I found Morbrecia's castle, no problem. The princess lives near the Dark Forest, on an island in the middle of a skreel-infested lake.

Skreel are deadly dangerous but I'm not afraid of them! I skim the water and land on a rocky ledge below a wall. Then I scan the castle with my laser-sharp eyes. In seconds I know the location of every door and window.

I spot my target! There's Morbrecia in a room downstairs. She's screaming orders at a servant. Excellent! She is exactly where I want her. I look around. No one in sight. Good! Time to get to work.

I draw a vial of *Steely Crystals* cobweb-spray from my tunic and aim it at a window . . . Soon the spider princess will be trapped in my cobwebs of steel!

*'m Nix!* My task is to track down the Outworlder, Sesame Brown. My master's memory spell tells me the troll in charge of Gate One knows a thing or two about her.

I'll go and see him first.

Ha! I took him completely by surprise.

131

He was having a nap, lazy thing! But he soon woke up when I twisted his beard.

"Tell me what Sesame looks like!" I demanded, twisting his beard tighter. And he described Sesame exactly.

Later, I came across some gribblers in the Dark Forest. A foul-smelling gribbler called Varg did all the talking - well, spitting more like! He told me about a couple of tunganoras who would know all about Sesame. So, I flew off in search of them.

I soon tracked down the ones I was looking for - a mother called Hob and her baby, Fig, living near Mount Fortuna. I hid behind a tree then ... I grabbed Fig and held him upside-down!

"Moomoo!" he squealed. I really frightened him.
Ha ha!

Hob was afraid of what I might do to her baby.
It didn't take her long to tell me everything she
knew about Sesame.

By now I reckoned I had enough news to
return and report to my master. But something
happened that day to change my plans . . .

Flying over River Two Moons, I see two girls fall
into the water. One of them is Sesame Brown!
Quick as a flash, I hide in a bush and overhear the
girls talking to the gatekeeper. Two Charmseekers! I
can't believe my luck! I decide to follow the girls and
tell Zorgan what they're up to. But as they pass my
hiding place, disaster strikes! My wings get caught on
a briar. I flap and struggle but it only makes matters
worse.

At last I manage to tear myself free, but now my
wings are torn and I've got to walk! I mustn't let
them out of my sight. If I fail in my
mission, I dread what my master will
do! I must hurry to catch up with
those Charmseekers . . .

# Seven

"There's a bridge,' said Sesame. "Let's cross and go into the Dark Forest. We can find our way to the palace from there."

Stepping from the light of the afternoon sun into the cool dark forest, the girls at once felt a sense of foreboding. It was strangely quiet among the trees, as they made their way along a narrow path. One side was flanked by the lower slopes of Mount Fortuna, where mossy boulders lay strewn about; on the other, wizened fir trees spread their slippery roots across the path. Sesame knew they were in a completely different part of the forest, from the last time she was there.

"I wish I'd asked Stanza for a map!" she told Maddy.

They hadn't been walking long when Sesame stopped dead in her tracks. A moment before, Maddy had been looking behind to investigate a rustle in the undergrowth and bumped straight into her.

"Ses! You might have . . ." she started to protest.

"Ssh! Listen," said Sesame.

"Singing!" said Maddy, surprised.

Out of the stillness the sound of singing floated through the trees.

"It's coming from over there," said Sesame. "Come on."

They fought their way through tangled roots, stopping every now and again to listen; the singing was definitely closer.

"There's something else," said Maddy, brushing a leafy twig from her face. "I'm sure I heard a horse neigh!"

"Me too," said Sesame. Then a few seconds later . . . "Look!"

A little way off, several riders on horseback were trotting along a wide track. Four uniformed guardsmen on shiny black horses surrounded a pure white horse, which was being ridden sidesaddle by a beautiful young woman. She wore a bright red riding jacket and skirt and in her long, flowing hair was a circlet of silver. They were all singing.

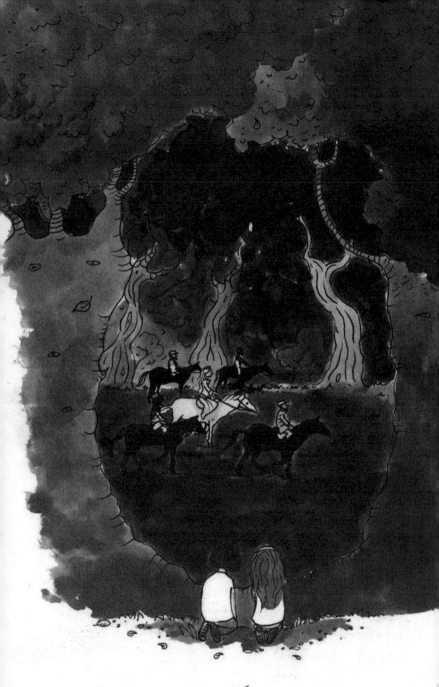

Sesame gasped.

"That must be Queen Charm," she whispered.

"Wow!" said Maddy.

And it was. Charm was on her way back to her palace from Mount Fortuna, following her visit to the Silver Pool with the Silversmith.

As Charm rode back through the forest, she had a lot on her mind. Only a few days ago she had visited some of the farmers whose crops had been ruined by floods. She had tried her best to comfort them but words didn't compensate for losing their valuable crops.

Everything was going wrong since the loss of her charm bracelet!

The thought of her bracelet reminded Charm of the song that had been sung at her coronation, when the Silversmith had first presented her with the magical charms. It had a lively tune and everyone knew the words, so she turned to her guardsmen and said:

"Come, let's sing the Song of Charms. It always makes me feel better!"

And they did.

Thirteen charms on a silver band,
United hold our world in hand.
May this gift for good Queen Charm,
Keep Karisma safe from harm.
One and all, beware the day
Charms and bracelet break away.
Together they must always stay!

Lantern, star and moon so bright,
Guide us through the darkest night.
Silver coin and lucky key,
Dolphin from the silvery sea,
Horseshoe, cat and clover too,
Fortune bring to me and you.
Nature's wonders please the eye;
Snowflake, shell and butterfly.
These precious charms should never part,
But be forever with the heart.

Sesame and Maddy were close enough to hear the words, as Charm and her escorts trotted by.

"It's all about the charms!" said Sesame, calling and waving with both hands, in the hope the queen might notice.

But Charm looked straight ahead and the cheerful singing drowned Sesame's shouts. Disappointed, the girls tumbled on to the grassy bridleway, now covered in fresh hoof prints.

"We can follow them to the palace!" said Maddy, as she watched the riders disappear round a bend. But before Sesame could reply, a shout came from a nearby tree:

"SESAME!"

Two tunganoras jumped down in front of her. It was Hob and Fig! Sesame was *so* pleased to see them,

she hugged them both at once. And when Maddy turned round, Sesame was lost in a mass of pink fur!

After Maddy had been introduced, it didn't take

Hob long to tell the girls all that had happened since she had last seen Sesame sprinting for the gate.

"I was so worried you'd get caught by that gribbler," said Sesame.

"I had him running round in circles!" said Hob. "He soon gave up."

Maddy cuddled Fig while they listened to Hob. When she came to the part about the pixie, Maddy looked up.

"I thought I saw something, as we were leaving Stanza!" she said. "An eye . . . something flapping . . . it might have been the pixie!"

Hob looked upset and began to cry.

"It's all my fault," she sobbed. "The pixie wanted to know all about you Sesame and I . . . I . . . told her everything I knew."

Sesame put her arm around Hob to comfort her.

"Don't worry," she said, "no wonder you were frightened with that horrid pixie threatening poor Fig. I'll deal with her, if I get the chance. You'll see!"

"Thank you," said Hob.

"But take care!"

Time was slipping by and Sesame was anxious to get to the palace and look for the charms. So, after many hugs and farewells, the girls hurried on their way.

And neither heard Nix, her footsteps light as snowflakes, following in their tracks . . .

# Eight

Morbrecia's screams of rage rang through the forest. She was a prisoner in her own castle! Trapped like a fly in a cobweb.

Dina had been quick to carry out her work, covering every door and window, every crevice and cranny in a mesh of steel. One vial of *STEELY CRYSTALS* cobweb-spray had been enough to seal the whole castle!

Inside there was pandemonium, as Morbrecia ordered her servants to tear down the barricades. But all to no avail; the mesh stuck fast to the outside and no amount of pulling or pushing would shift it.

"This is Zorgan's work!" ranted Morbrecia, pacing up and down like a caged animal.

She stopped by a window and peered through the latticed screen. She could see Charm's palace, away in the distance.

"Or perhaps my dear little sister has discovered *I* stole her precious bracelet," she fumed. "This is all her doing! Or maybe . . ."

The last word trailed off as another possibility struck Morbrecia. She clenched her fists and stamped her foot.

"That Outworlder!" she hissed. "If Sesame Brown has been foolish enough to return. . . if *she's* responsible for this outrage – she'll be sorry! No one crosses me and gets away with it. Ever!"

For some time, Sesame and Maddy had been following the trail of hoof prints. Now they had reached the edge of the forest, where River Two Moons wound its way lazily towards a lake with a castle. The ground was marshy by the river and the track soon vanished. As the late afternoon sun slipped down through the trees, Sesame realised to her dismay there wasn't much time left and they hadn't even reached Charm's palace.

"It's getting late and we haven't found any charms!" she wailed.

"When do we have to be at the gate?" asked Maddy.

"Moonrise," said Sesame. "Whenever *that* is." She checked her watch and was delighted to see the dial had mysteriously changed, to show Karisma time. It had happened once before.

The girls paused briefly to see how it worked. And then came a piercing yell.

"What was that?" exclaimed Maddy.

"It came from the castle," said Sesame.

"Sounds like someone"s in trouble," said Maddy.

"Mmm," said Sesame, with a sigh of despair. She was torn between her mission to look for the charms, or helping someone in distress! But she decided they had to investigate. "Let's see if we can help," she said.

The girls squelched their way through the boggy marsh to a bridge, which was the only way across the lake. The castle loomed dark and forbidding before them, and they saw immediately that every door and window was covered in a fine steely mesh. Sesame and Maddy could see no way of getting in or out.

"What now?" said Maddy, as another high-pitched screech pierced the air.

They looked up and saw the shadowy figure of a woman, her hair flying behind her, at the top of a tower. It was Morbrecia. She had spotted them from the battlements. Sesame and Maddy waved, but Morbrecia returned their friendly gesture with a snarl.

"Balam✱ Outworlders!" she bellowed. "Think you can defeat me, huh? Well, you're mistaken! I'll have you thrown in the lake. You'll be skreel meals in no time!"

"Oh, n-nice," said Sesame, trembling at Morbrecia's threatening tone.

* * * * * * * * * * * * * * * * * * * * * * * * * * * * *

✱**Balam** – cursed, an angry exclamation

145

"Who is she?" whispered Maddy, cowering beside her. "What are we supposed to have done?"

Before Sesame could answer, the terrible whiff of rotting fish filled the air.

"Urrrrgh!" said Maddy, holding her nose.

"Oh no!" groaned Sesame, her stomach churning at the thought of what it could be. And when she turned around, she was confronted with her worst nightmare . . .

Standing on the far side of the bridge, blocking their way, stood a gang of gribblers – led by the biggest one, Varg.

Maddy screamed and clung to Sesame. Slowly Varg began to make his way towards them, dribbling slimy goo.

"Ssheshame Brown!" he sneered, drawing his thin, lizard lips over yellowing teeth. "At lasht!"

For a moment, Sesame and Maddy were rooted to the spot, frozen with fear. Then a blood-curdling yell from Morbrecia distracted Varg.

"Don't just stand there, magworts! Grab them! Move! Now! And get me out of here!"

After that, many things happened at once.

Sesame grabbed Maddy's hand and they leaped off the bridge, on to some rocks at the foot of the castle. The gribblers gave chase, lumbering over the bridge, grunting like pigs, while Morbrecia cursed them for being too slow. And Nix, who had been stealthily following Sesame and Maddy on foot, suddenly found herself trampled by gribblers!

"Ooof! Ow! Ouch!" she squealed. She stank of fish and was covered in slime. Nix knew she was beaten this time. She slunk away to return to Zorgan's Tower and face the wrath of her master.

Meanwhile Sesame and Maddy were nimbly leaping from one large rock to another, water lapping at their feet. Every so often they caught sight of a small, sharp fin, slicing the surface of the lake . . .

Rounding a corner of the castle they lost sight of the gribblers, now scrabbling about on the rocks; they were in danger of becoming a snack for the skreel. The girls stopped for a minute, to get their breath. And suddenly there it was.

"Oh, Maddy!" Sesame cried. "Look!"

There, glistening on a stone by her foot, was a tiny silver horseshoe.

"Ses!" yelled Maddy excitedly. "You found a charm!"

"*We!*" corrected Sesame, hastily stooping to pick it up. She held it in the palm of her hand – a perfect miniature horseshoe, with the tiniest holes for silver nails.

"And I'm going to have it!" said a cruel voice right behind them.

The girls wheeled round to face a pixie with flaming red hair and bright, crystal eyes. She stood there, threatening them with a vial of *Steely Crystals*. It was Dina.

"Hand over that charm!" she demanded.

"No way!" said Sesame, quickly recovering from her surprise at seeing the pixie. She clenched the horseshoe tightly in her fist. She felt fiercely protective of the newly-found charm, now strangely warm in her hand. This was why she'd come. Finding the horseshoe was meant to be!

"Give it to me," hissed Dina, "or—"

"—or what?" cut in Maddy.

"I'll spray you with this!" said Dina. "You saw what it did to the castle?"

They had. And they were in no doubt that Dina would take great pleasure in giving them the same treatment. Adding to their plight, they could hear the gribblers puffing and panting, getting closer by the minute. And the stench was simply dreadful.

"Let's swim for it!" Sesame whispered to Maddy,

quickly putting the horseshoe in her pocket. She refused to give it up!

But Dina heard her.

"You won't get far," she said. "The lake is full of skreel. They'll eat you in a grickle!"*

Sesame looked and saw the flash of a fin. She remembered Morbrecia's threat, too, and knew Dina was right. But it was their only way of escape. The two moons of Karisma were already in the sky; before long it would be moonrise. They had to risk it and fast!

Just then Maddy spotted some plants that, with the rising of the moons, were appearing on the surface of the lake. Giant moon-lilies were popping up everywhere, their huge lily pads floating on the water – like stepping stones . . .

* * * * * * * * * * * * * * * * * * * * * * * * * * * *

*Grickle – about the same time as a second in our world

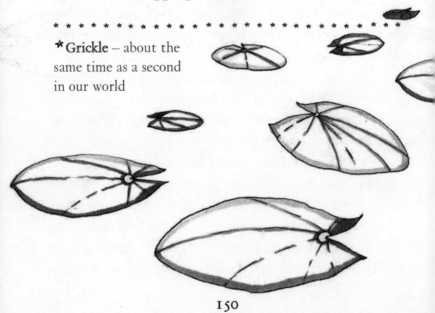

"RUN!" said Maddy, grabbing Sesame and pulling her over the rocks. "Run for your life!"

Thrown off guard, Dina lost her balance. She aimed a jet of *Steely Crystals* at the girls, but missed and caught two gribblers, binding them in a web of steel. And as Varg lumbered into sight, Dina flew off as fast as her wings could carry her.

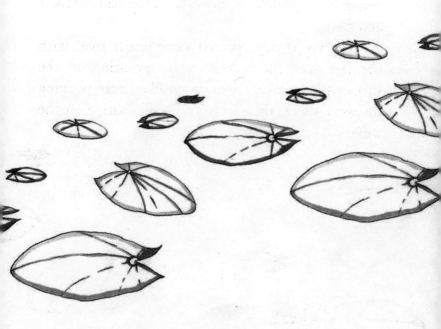

The Charmseekers must cross Morbrecia's lake which is filled with flesh—eating skreel! Can you help them find a safe way across the water?

The Chainseekers must cross Mothbrecia lake, which is filled with flesh-eating skreel. Can you help them find a safe way across the water?

# Nine

Maddy led the way, springing from one moon-lily pad to another, with Sesame close behind. Beneath them the water frothed and foamed; the razor-toothed skreel worked themselves into a feeding frenzy and leapt out to snap at their heels. But, at last, the girls jumped to safety. As they pelted away, the sound of Morbrecia's curses echoed across the lake; the gribblers were afraid of the skreel and had given up the chase. No words could describe her fury.

But now the enemy was Time! Sesame snatched a look at her watch. The two moons in the centre of

the dial were moving steadily into position, above Mount Fortuna. When they were directly over the peak, it would be moonrise.

Together the girls raced along a path by the river – luckily, on the right side for the gate. They could see Stanza waiting for them, and sparkling pin pricks of light all around the bush.

"Run! Run!" Stanza shouted, his hoof pawing the ground.

And as the two moons of Karisma settled over the peak of the mountain – Sesame and Maddy dived headfirst into the silvery mist and through the gate . . .

"There, all done!" said the farrier, wiping his hands on his leather apron. Silver was standing proudly, displaying four new shoes.

"Good boy!" said Jodie, patting the pony's neck and giving him a titbit. "Sesame, could you lead Silver back to the stable for me? And Maddy, would you fill a hay net please?"

"Er . . .yeah," said Sesame, swaying.

"Hay . . . what?" said Maddy, dazed and confused.

Jodie looked concerned.

"You okay girls?" she asked.

"Fine!" said Sesame, shaking her head and brushing silver sparkles from her eyelashes. "We're fine, aren't we Maddy?"

Maddy nodded. She was still seeing stars.

"Mmm," she said.

"Here," said Jodie, picking up one of Silver's cast-off shoes and giving it to Sesame. "For luck!"

"Thanks!" said Sesame, with a beaming smile. "Come on, Silver!"

✳ ✳ ✳

Later, upstairs in Sesame's room, the girls sat on her bed and talked about everything that had happened that day. The jewellery box lay open on Sesame's bedside table; inside were Queen Charm's bracelet and now there were two charms – the heart and the horseshoe – side by side.

"I still can't believe we've been there," said Maddy. "It all seems like a dream."

"But it's REAL!" said Sesame, her brown eyes wide with excitement. "And we went to Karisma together! We're a team, Maddy, like we said we would be, remember?"

"Yes!" said Maddy. "Best friends and . . ."

"Charmseekers!" said Sesame. "We're in this together now. It's our secret. You mustn't tell anyone. Not yet. Promise?"

Maddy nodded. "Promise," she said, crossing two fingers and pointing them down – their secret sign for *I'll keep my word*. Then she joked: "Anyway, no one would believe me, if I did!"

They laughed, but Sesame was suddenly serious. There were still eleven empty places on the tray in the jewellery box – each waiting to be filled with a missing charm. Maddy knew exactly what Sesame was thinking.

"Do you think you'll find them all, Ses?" she asked, quietly.

Sesame looked at Maddy with an expression of fierce determination.

"I've *got* to," she said, gently closing the lid of the box. "I'm a Charmseeker. I can't give up till I've found every one!"

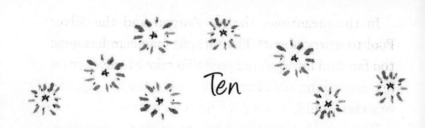

# Ten

The Silversmith smiles to herself, as a candle flickers and dies. She knows another precious charm has been found, for it is the candle that bears its name that has just gone out. Ah, it is the little horseshoe! And now she "sees" it is safe with Sesame and together with the heart.

Eleven of the thirteen magic candles glow and each of them will burn brightly until its charm has been found – no matter how long it takes. And in time they *will* be found, of that she feels sure. Out of all the terrible things that have happened since the bracelet has been stolen, the Silversmith knows she can rely on Sesame Brown to do her best. There will come a day when all thirteen charms are united, returned to Queen Charm where they belong . . .

158

In the meantime, there's Zorgan and the Silver Pool to worry about! That stupid magician has gone too far. And for what purpose? To take his revenge on her for making the bracelet? To spite her because the bracelet wouldn't work for him?

Well, she has managed to save one precious cup of silver! An idea has been forming in her head – something perhaps she should have thought about moons ago! There is a chance she can resolve the situation and calm the spirit of Agapogo, which Zorgan has so cruelly used.

But that is another story. It must be told another day!

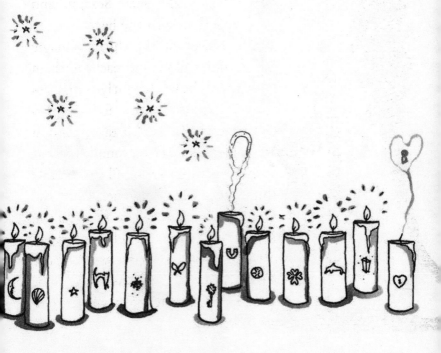

# The Dragon's Revenge

For Tom, with love.
A.T.

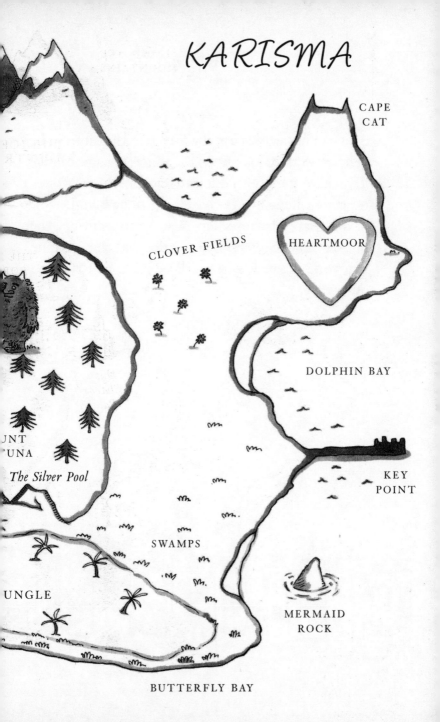

Alone in her workshop, the Silversmith pauses in her delicate work to look upon the thirteen magic candles. Two have gone out. Eleven remain lit, each one a beacon of hope for its charm, yet to be found.

Will her Charmseeker return, to continue her quest? The Silversmith smiles as she resumes her work. Sesame Brown will be back, of that she is quite sure!

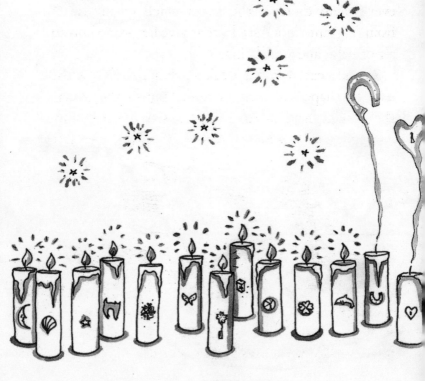

# One

The Silversmith's workshop lies at the foot of Mount Fortuna, not far from the Silver Pool. Inside is a wonderful collection of curious objects, carvings, sculptures and ornaments that fire her imagination for her own beautiful creations. It is here she once cast the magical charm bracelet! And everywhere there is the sweet smell of mystica* from fragrant tinder-sticks that give her workshop an air of calm and well-being.

Spread neatly on her workbench are the tools she uses to shape, cast, engrave and polish the things she makes. And amid all these sits a small cup, containing a precious measure of silver, the last

* * * * * * * * * * * * * * * * * * * * * * * * * *

*Mystica* — an aromatic plant, native to Karisma. The petals produce a sweet smell when burned

167

drops she saved from the Silver Pool.

For many long days the Silversmith has been busy making a new crown. She works with infinite care and skill, hoping there will be just enough silver to finish it. She vividly recalls every moment of her mission to rescue what little remained of the Silver Pool. It happened not long ago . . .

On that particular day I had taken Queen Charm to the Silver Pool. We had both been horrified to see how quickly the pool was losing silver. After Queen Charm had gone, I returned and, summoning all my courage, I called upon the spirit of Agapogo. All at once a wind blew up and the force of it knocked me back. Then the ghostly vision of Agapogo appeared and looked so angry that at first I was afraid.

But I spoke softly to Agapogo to calm her unhappy spirit.

"You have every reason to be angry," I said. "Zorgan has used his magic powers selfishly. You have been cursed to drain this precious pool for one purpose. So he can take his revenge on me!"

At the mention of Zorgan's name, Agapogo snorted and the air was filled with scalding steam.

"Zorgan is guilty of recklessly wasting the silver. But I must confess that I, and probably countless Silversmiths before me, have drawn silver from this pool without thinking it would ever run out. We've taken it for granted. We've always assumed the magical pool would refill, no matter how much silver was used. So we have been foolish too, Agapogo.

However, if you allow me one last measure of silver I will make amends, I promise. And you will be honoured throughout Karisma."

Agapogo's massive form glowed eerily and at last I heard her spirit sigh, as if some heavy burden had been lifted from her.

"Oh, Silversmith, good Silversmith,
Your words of wisdom ease my pain.
Your skillful craft has always been
In honour of our noble queen.
May your promise break this curse,
And Zorgan's evil plan reverse!"

Then Agapogo disappeared and I was left marvelling at the dragon's words. Taking a ladle, I scooped up the last drops of silver, poured them into a cup and took it safely back to my workshop . . .

Now the Silversmith twists the last few filigree strands of her design, turning it round and round to inspect her new creation.

"There is still one drop of silver left," she declares.

It was all part of her plan. And, if it worked, all would be well.

"The Crown of Agapogo!" exclaimed Queen Charm, examining every exquisite detail of the silver circlet. "Oh, it's beautiful! And you've used sparkling rubies for the eyes. Perfect!"

"Thank you, Your Majesty," said the Silversmith, delighted Charm was so pleased with her work. "I took the greatest care when casting it. I had only one precious cupful of silver to make it. In fact, I used all but one drop!"

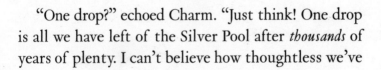

"One drop?" echoed Charm. "Just think! One drop is all we have left of the Silver Pool after *thousands* of years of plenty. I can't believe how thoughtless we've been not to remember Agapogo for her priceless legacy, until now." The queen placed the crown carefully on her head, trying it for size. "It is lovely," she said, "but it can never take the place of my charm bracelet."

"Why, of course not," said the Silversmith. "Nothing will ever take the place of the magical charms. Until they are found, we remain in peril. The crown is merely a token of our respect for Agapogo, after so many years of neglect."

"Will Agapogo be appeased?" asked Charm. "Will she know you sacrificed the last of the silver in her honour?"

"I believe so," said the Silversmith. "Perhaps you could wear the crown on a special occasion?"

Charm thought for a moment.

"I have it!" she announced. "I shall declare a holiday. It will be known as Agapogo Day!"

The Silversmith smiled.

"That is a very good idea, Your Majesty," she said.

## Two

Zorgan was pleased with himself. Only the most powerful sorcerer could make Agapogo drain the Silver Pool.

"You checked the pool as I ordered?" Zorgan shot the question at his pixies hovering nearby.

"Yes, Master," said Nix. "We flew right to the bottom. It was very, very hot down there!"

"We couldn't find any silver," confirmed Dina. "Not a drop!"

"Good, good," said Zorgan.

He stood stroking his pet bandrall*, Vanda, imagining, with considerable relish, the horrified look that must have crossed the

* * * * * * * * * * * * * *

*Bandrall* – rare flying mammal, native to Karisma

176

Silversmith's face when she'd discovered the empty pool.

A sharp pain in his wrist jolted Zorgan back to reality. He rubbed the scar where once, for a fleeting moment, he had worn the fabulous charm bracelet, the bracelet that could never be his! He was sure the Silversmith had enchanted it, causing it to burn him so cruelly. Well, he'd had his revenge. His thin lips twisted in a sneer.

"Serves her right!" he said. "But now I must attend to a more urgent matter. Sesame Brown!"

The sorcerer knew all about Sesame's last visit to Karisma, the pixies had given him a full report, but he'd been furious with them for allowing Sesame to escape with another charm.

"We must find a way to stop her coming here again," he told Vanda, gently placing her on a perch. "Hm! I have an idea . . ."

Zorgan hurried to the Star Room to consult his crystal ball. In the dim light, the sphere glowed eerily like a moon. Zorgan peered into the shimmering mist, swirling around inside. Would the magic work? Would it be powerful enough to take him far beyond the reaches of Karisma to the

Outworld? It was worth a try. There was urgency in his voice as he intoned:

*"Take me now through time and space,*
*That I may see the Seeker's face;*
*Oh mystic powers reveal to me,*
*The one I seek is - Sesame!"*

Slowly the mist cleared. At first there was nothing. Then, gradually, a picture of blue sky and sea appeared. Seconds went by. Zorgan drummed his fingers impatiently on the glass.

"Come on, come on!" he growled.

The image faded, a small white cottage appeared, wavered and changed to show an odd-shaped room, then suddenly a girl's smiling face swam into view. Zorgan could barely contain his excitement. It must be Sesame. He fixed his cold black eyes on her.

"Vermy* Outworlder!** You'll never come here again, you, you—"

Zorgan controlled himself. The vision wouldn't last for long and there was hardly any time left to cast the spell. Hastily he began to chant:

*"Shades and shadows cloud your eyes-"* but got no further, before a blinding flash lit up the Star Room.

* * * * * * * * * * * * * * * * * * * * * * * * *

* **Vermy** – a miserable worm

** **Outworlder** – the name Karismans call someone from our world

When Zorgan had recovered from the shock, when he looked once more into the crystal ball, Sesame had gone! She had simply vanished into thin air and, try as he might, Zorgan could not bring her back.

Zorgan was livid. The mist refused to clear. It seemed as if another, more powerful force was present — an invisible, protective shield was clouding his vision of Sesame.

"I *will* find a way to stop her," he promised himself. "It is only a matter of time."

# Three

"I won't see my favourite pony for two whole weeks!" groaned Sesame. She was talking to her riding instructor, Jodie Luck.

Jodie had found Sesame in the stable, saying goodbye to Silver. It was the start of the summer holidays and Sesame had spent the day helping with the ponies.

"Of course!" said Jodie, remembering something Sesame had mentioned earlier. "You're going away tomorrow aren't you?"

"Yes," said Sesame. "We're going to Cornwall. Lossy and Maddy are coming. I wish you could come too."

Jodie smiled.

"Thank you," she said, touched by Sesame's warmth. "But who would take care of the ponies?"

"Mmm," said Sesame, stroking Silver's nose. "Someone has to look after *you*!"

Silver gave a friendly snort, as if he understood every word.

"Is Lossy your mum?" asked Jodie.

"No, she's my gran," said Sesame. "Mum died when I was a baby."

"Sorry," said Jodie.

"That's OK," said Sesame. "Poppy, that's my mum, died in a car crash. I live with——"

Just then, Nic Brown arrived to take Sesame home.

"Hi Dad!" she said, giving Silver one last hug.

Jodie and Nic had met once before. Jodie remembered his twinkling, nut-brown eyes.

"Hello," she said, blushing. "Sesame was just telling me about——"

At that moment her mobile rang and she fished it out of her pocket.

"Who? Oh, yes. Friday will be fine—"

She broke off to mouth "sorry" to Nic and "have a good time" to Sesame, before continuing.

"Bye," said Nic, wishing he could stay longer.

As they were walking to the car, Sesame couldn't help noticing how happy he looked.

"I think Jodie's great," she remarked, casually.

"Mmm," said Nic. "So do I . . ."

Sesame spotted it first.

"Look!" she cried. "The sea!"

There was a cheer from the others in the car. Nic, Lossy, Sesame and Maddy had been driving down a twisty Cornish lane, flanked by windblown trees and banks of wildflowers. Rounding a corner they saw a

small white cottage perched on a hill. It had a yellow front door and a thatched roof; beyond was a sandy cove and the blue Atlantic Ocean. Nic stopped the car.

"Cliff Cottage, Dad?" queried Sesame, reading the name on the gate.

Nic checked the holiday brochure.

"Yes," he said. "And that's Gullhilly Cove."

"Marvellous!" said Lossy. "Let's go in."

The cottage was very cosy. It had low-beamed ceilings and brightly-coloured rugs on the floors. Upstairs were three lovely bedrooms. When Sesame

discovered the smallest, she called Maddy to come and see it.

"This is ours!" she said.

It was an odd-shaped room with a latticed window beneath the eaves and two beds with patchwork quilts. Maddy came in and dumped her case on the floor.

"Fab!" she said.

Quickly the girls unpacked. Maddy put her things away neatly in a drawer, Sesame stuffed hers in anyhow, except for the last item, which she placed carefully by her bed. It was her jewellery box. Maddy looked surprised.

"You brought it?" she said.

"Of course," said Sesame, lifting the lid to check that the beautiful silver bracelet and the heart and horseshoe charms were in place. She dropped her voice to a whisper. "If we go to Karisma and find another charm, I'll have to keep it safe, won't I?"

"Right," said Maddy. "You really believe we're going back?"

Sesame hesitated for a moment before answering. She wondered if she *would* find a way to Karisma. Supposing she could *never* go there again! Her tummy did a backwards flip. She felt wobbly. Maddy was looking at her in a funny way.

"What's up, Ses?" she asked.

"N-n-nothing," said Sesame. "I felt a bit strange. But I'm fine now."

"Karisma?" prompted Maddy.

"Yes," said Sesame. "We'll get there somehow!"

She looked inside her jewellery box again before closing the lid.

"Eleven charms are still missing, remember? Sesame Brown will track them down!"

Just then Lossy popped her head round the door.

"Anyone for the beach?" she said.

# Four

Agapogo was free at last. The Silversmith had broken Zorgan's curse, just in time to save the Silver Pool. Now Agapogo was thirsty for revenge on the wicked magician.

Entering a cavern at the heart of Mount Fortuna, the dragon spectre looked around. Ghostly eyes glowed like red-hot coals and, in a while, Agapogo spotted the mound. There, heaped upon the sandy floor, was a clutch of eggs with purple spots. They were unmistakably drakon* eggs!

There are few who would not shudder at the very mention of a drakon. Dragon bugs (as they are commonly known) shoot flames from their jaws and are among the largest, most dangerous insects in

* * * * * * * * * * * * * * * * * * * * * * * * * * *

* **Drakon** – a large, fire-breathing insect

Karisma. Farmers especially fear them, for a drakoon* of fire-breathing drakons can destroy a crop of clover in no time!

Now these particular eggs had been laid a long time ago. The mother had hidden them deep inside the cavern, where she knew they would be safe. It could be years before the temperature was just right for her young to hatch, because drakon eggs require heat – intense heat – and Agapogo knew that too.

"My beauties!" Agapogo whispered tenderly, as if the eggs were her own. "Your time has come!"

Then she took the deepest breath and filled her nostrils with a headwind from the East, a tailwind from the West, a gale from the North and a hurricane from the South. When she was full to bursting she ROARED! And the force of her breath was like a scorching whirlwind. Sparks whizzed round like Catherine wheels, until they were spinning so fast that they turned into a massive ball of fire. Then the fireball blasted its way up through a crack in the mountain and burst out of the top with an ear-splitting

## BANG!

* * * * * * * * * * * * * * * * * * * * * * * * * * * * * *

*Drakoon* – collective name for a large number of drakons

It was as if a thousand fireworks had exploded at once!

Meanwhile, the heat in the cavern grew hotter and hotter. When it was as hot as a furnace, the eggs split open.

CRACK! CRACK! CRACK!

One by one the drakons emerged from their splintered shells. Before long, there was a drakoon of dragon bugs spitting fire and ready to fly!

Agapogo spoke to them in Dracodictum*, the language of dragons, which the drakons understood perfectly.

"Drakons rise, your wings unfold,
The time has come, you must be bold.
To Zorgan's Tower, my fiery friends,
I need your help to make amends.
Yes, haste to where the wizard dwells
And there you'll find his books of spells.
Feast on these and take your fill
To satisfy my vengeful will!"

*Dracodictum* – the language of dragons

As soon as Agapogo finished speaking, the drakons unfolded their wings, glowing with flaming colours – blue, orange and red. In the next instant, the air was alive with wildly fluttering drakons soaring up through the vent. They poured from the top of Mount Fortuna and, like fiery locusts, swarmed towards Zorgan's Tower.

## Five

The first week of the holiday went by in a flash. Every day Sesame and Maddy went swimming or sightseeing with Nic and Lossy; and sometimes the girls went shopping on their own, at the little fishing village nearby.

One day Sesame wore her red top with the sparkly heart and put on her favourite necklace – the locket with pictures of Nic and Poppy inside. As she fastened the clasp Sesame felt a tingle at the nape of her neck and, in that moment, any doubts she'd had about returning to Karisma simply faded away. She didn't know why, but she had a feeling today was going to be special!

After breakfast they all walked down the winding cliff path to Gullhilly Cove. Nic had planned to spend the morning surfing and had brought his board.

"Should catch some good ones today," he said, scrutinising the waves. "See you later!"

"Bye, Dad. Don't fall off!" Sesame called after him, as he went to join a group of surfers. Then she turned to Maddy. "Come on. Let's explore."

"Have fun," said Lossy, settling down to read her book. "But stay where I can see you."

"We will," the girls promised, as they ran off across the beach. For a while they were absorbed peering into rock pools, finding tiny crabs, starfish and pretty pebbles as they wandered further and further along the beach.

"Maybe we should go back now?" suggested Maddy, looking around anxiously for Sesame's gran. Lossy was nowhere in sight, but she saw Nic, splashing around in the surf. "Oh! Your dad's just fallen off his board!"

Sesame goggled her eyes.

"Trust Dad," she said.

She was about to follow Maddy, when she came across a cave at the foot of the cliff.

"Wait!" she cried. "I'm going to have a look in here."

Maddy scrambled over the rocks after her.

"Ooo," she said, peering into the gloomy cavern. "It's really spooky!"

Her voice echoed round the walls and came ringing back, to mock her.

SPOOOKY OOOKY OOOKY!

"It's OK," said Sesame, walking in boldly. Almost immediately her eye caught something bright, sparkling above her head and, glancing up, she gave a gasp of surprise. "Maddy! Come here. This is amazing."

"What is?" said Maddy, taking a few hesitant paces inside. She felt cold and afraid.

"Look at these shells," said Sesame. "There must be hundreds of them!"

And so there were. The roof of the cave was studded with glistening, silvery fossils, shimmering with a translucent light of their own. For a second or two, Sesame and Maddy stood gazing at them. Then, almost without thinking, they started walking along the narrow passageway, following the luminous trail of shells, until Sesame stopped dead in her tracks.

"Wh-what?" whispered Maddy.

"There," said Sesame, pointing to a spot ahead of them. "A red light. Waving about. See?"

Maddy looked over Sesame's shoulder and froze. She was convinced it was a terrible, red-eyed monster.

"I'm really scared, Ses. Let's go."

But Sesame took her by the arm. She felt drawn towards the flickering light and walked slowly forward.

"Stay close to me," she told Maddy. "It'll be all right. I've got the weirdest feeling—"

She broke off because the rippling light suddenly burst into a shower of silvery stars.

"Wow!" cried the girls together.

And next thing they knew they were floating, tumbling, falling through a thousand twinkling stars into another world . . .

## Six

# BOOM!

Zorgan was in his Star Room when he heard the thud of an explosion. The air shook. The tower shuddered.

"Quisto!"* he exclaimed. "What was that?"

The pixies, Nix and Dina, heard it too. Sensing their master was in danger, they immediately flew to his side. Vanda flew round in circles, screeching.

In the distance Zorgan saw smoke billowing from Mount Fortuna.

"Extraordinary," he murmured, half-fascinated, half-fearful of this unusual happening. Mount Fortuna had never erupted before. Why now?

Nix and Dina surveyed the scene.

"Look, Master," said Nix, pointing to a dark, sinister-looking cloud, silhouetted against the sky.

The magician narrowed his eyes, scanning the horizon.

"Debris" concluded Zorgan. "Smuts from the smoke."

* * * * * * * * * * * * * * * * * * * * * * * * * * * *

*Quisto – an exclamation of surprise

196

"No, Master," said Nix, setting her eyeball lenses to 'zoom'. Her cold, crystal eyes glinted with excitement. "Bugs!"

"Spitting fire!" added Dina.

Zorgan looked again. The cloud was heading towards them fast, countless flaming lights moving and weaving as one.

"Identify!" he barked.

"Drakons!" chorused the pixies.

"Shut the tower!" yelled Zorgan. "We're under attack!"

Nix and Dina raced around the tower slamming windows and doors. But the speed of the advancing drakons took them all by surprise. A cluster came hurtling against a window –

# CRASH!

– smashing the glass into a thousand pieces. Within seconds the Star Room was alive with fire-spewing bugs. Flasks and test tubes shattered in their fiery breath and foul-smelling potions spilled on the floor.

Zorgan uttered the first insect-zapping curse he could think of.

"STUPIFLY!" he cried, pointing his wand at a passing drakon. But the curse missed the bug, backfired and singed his beard.

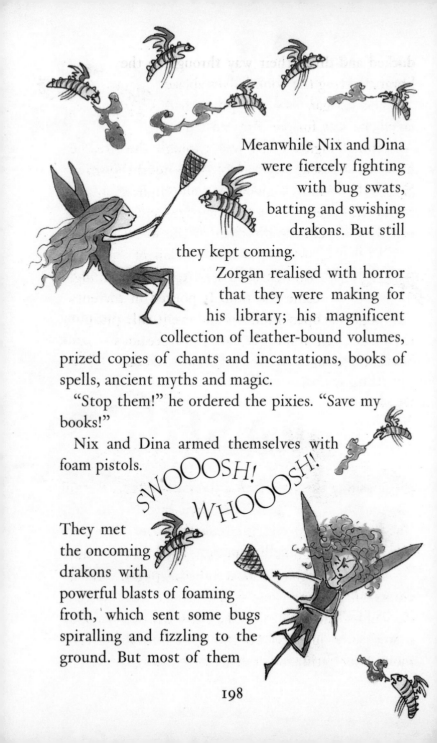

Meanwhile Nix and Dina were fiercely fighting with bug swats, batting and swishing drakons. But still they kept coming.

Zorgan realised with horror that they were making for his library; his magnificent collection of leather-bound volumes, prized copies of chants and incantations, books of spells, ancient myths and magic.

"Stop them!" he ordered the pixies. "Save my books!"

Nix and Dina armed themselves with foam pistols.

SWOOOSH! WHOOOSH!

They met the oncoming drakons with powerful blasts of foaming froth, which sent some bugs spiralling and fizzling to the ground. But most of them ducked and dived their way through to the library, setting the bookshelves ablaze.

When Zorgan saw the pixies had failed, he was furious. He must do something! Fighting his way through the fire, he managed to rescue a volume of **Advanced Weather Spells** by Windy Doldrums, only slightly singed round the edges. He flipped the pages and, finding a useful rain spell, rapidly chanted the words.

After a deafening clap of thunder and a streak of lightning, came the rain. It poured in torrents through the open windows and eventually put out the flames. All around lay Zorgan's precious books, their pages charred and rain-soaked.

Then an odd thing happened. Letters and words began to float off the pages. Spells, curses and incantations – indeed the very words Zorgan had chanted to invoke the spirit of Agapogo – were now jumbled up and spiralling about the room. Worse still, the drakons were eating them!

At last, when they had eaten their fill, the bugs flew away leaving Zorgan in the ruins of his once beautiful library.

"This is Agapogo's doing!" he shouted. "She sent those balam* bugs here. I'll get my own back, you'll see. Now, you useless pixies, clear up this mess!"

* * * * * * * * * * * * * * * * * * * * * * * * * * * *

**Balam** – cursed, an angry exclamation

# Seven

Sesame and Maddy tumbled through the air like clothes in a washing machine. Suddenly, they dropped straight down and landed on a pile of feathers. Unfortunately, the feathers belonged to Feenix the firebird, who shot into the air with a terrified SQUAWK!

Sesame and Maddy went sprawling.

"Flaming Fizzwigs!" cried Feenix. "Mind where you plonk yourselves!"

The girls stood up. An enormous bird with magnificent red and gold plummage was glaring at them. She looked most annoyed.

"Sorry," said Sesame, brushing a feather off her nose. "We didn't *mean* to land on you."

"Couldn't help it," added Maddy.

Feenix eyed them inquisitively, uttering "Ah!" and "Hm!" every now and again. Then something must have clicked, because suddenly she greeted them enthusiastically.

"Sesame Brown? Maddy Webb? Charmseekers from the Outworld?"* she asked.

"Right," replied Sesame.

"That's us," said Maddy.

"Oh, my!" said Feenix. "I've heard all about you Charmseekers. And here you are at my gate. I'm Feenix. Gatekeeper Three. Welcome to Karisma!"

Sesame and Maddy looked at each other. They felt as famous as pop stars! Looking around they saw they were standing by a wrought-iron gate set in a wall and, through the ironwork, they could make out a street.

"Where are we?" asked Sesame.

"Lantern Hill," replied Feenix. "There's a carnival here today. It's Agapogo Day."

## ☆ AGAPOGO DAY ☆
Her Majesty Queen Charm has proclaimed that today shall be a holiday, to be celebrated throughout Karisma, in honour of Agapogo, the Dragon of the Silver Pool.
By Royal Command

☆

* * * * * * * * * * * * * * * * * * * * * * * * * *

* Outworld — the name Karismans call our world

"Sounds fun!" said Sesame. "But we're here to look for the missing charms."

"How long have we got?" asked Maddy.

"Be back before the bell strikes three," warned Feenix.

"Come on, Maddy," said Sesame. "Let's go."

The two set off down a narrow street hung with lanterns and paper dragons. The air felt chilly as they walked along and when some warmly-dressed Karismans gave them quizzical looks, Sesame and Maddy realised they were still dressed for the beach.

"We must look totally bonkers!" said Sesame. "It's winter here."

"I've got goose-bumps," complained Maddy, vigorously rubbing her arms.

Turning a corner at the end of the street, they came to a busy market. It was full of gaily decorated carts and stalls with traders shouting their wares. Soon Sesame and Maddy found themselves being jostled along past rows of stallholders selling dragon cakes, masks, lanterns and lollipops. And everywhere people were enjoying themselves and getting ready for the carnival that night.

"This is crazy," said Maddy, squeezing past a hairy

troll selling firecrackers. "We won't find any charms here. Let's try somewhere else."

"OK," agreed Sesame. "Lead the way!"

She was about to follow Maddy through the market, when

CRICK-CRACK! WEEEEEEEEEEEEE!

A fizzing firecracker shot past her. The hairy troll had set one off for fun! Sesame saw the firework land by a girl selling pots and potions from a tray. Before Sesame could shout a warning –

**BANG!** The cracker went off in a shower of sparks. The startled girl tipped up her tray and everything fell at her feet.

"Doofer!"* she yelled at the troll, who seemed to think it was very funny. "I hate trolls!" She burst into tears.

Straightaway Sesame went to comfort her.

"Don't cry," she said. "I'll help you."

Together they gathered up all the bottles, pots and jars. The girl was dressed in green and Sesame noticed she had a pair of wings folded neatly down her back. She was a fairy!  When she saw Sesame looking at her, she smiled.

"I'm Quilla," she said. "And you're the Seeker from the Outworld, aren't you?"

"Yes," said Sesame, quite surprised. "Sesame Brown. And this is my friend—"

She stopped, remembering she should have been following Maddy. Sesame looked around but Maddy was nowhere in sight.

"I must go, Quilla," she said, urgently.

* * * * * * * * * * * * * * * * * * * * * * * * * * * *

*Doofer* – idiot of the first order, brainless

"Here, take this," said Quilla, handing her a pot.

"What is it?" asked Sesame.

"Vanishing Cream," said Quilla. "To thank you for helping me. Works like magic. You may need it sooner than you think! Setfair*, Seeker."

"Thanks!" said Sesame, wondering what she meant. But she was worried about Maddy, so putting the pot in her pocket, she hurried away.

Meanwhile Maddy was waiting anxiously near the market. She was sure Sesame had been right behind her. She was about to look for her when a woman

* Setfair – goodbye and good luck

with wild, black hair grabbed her shoulder. Most of her face was hidden behind a mask. All Maddy saw were bright red lips, curled in an icy smile.

"Waiting for someone?" enquired the woman sweetly. But there was a chilling edge to her tone.

"Er . . . yes," said Maddy.

The woman took a step closer.

"Who? I may be able to help?"

"My-my friend, Ses-sesame," stammered Maddy, desperately wishing Ses would appear.

"Ssssssesameee!" hissed the woman, like a snake spitting venom. "Well, why don't we look for *Sesame* together!"

It was not a question. The woman had Maddy's arm in a vice-like grip.

"Come along—"

"No!" cried Maddy, wrenching herself free as she caught sight of Sesame.

"Ses! Ses! I'm here!" she yelled.

Sesame could see she looked upset.

"I'm really sorry," she said. "I stopped to—"

But Maddy wasn't listening.

"Did you see her?" she said.

"Who?" asked Sesame.

"That woman in a mask!" said Maddy, pointing.

But when they looked, the woman was nowhere to be seen. Maddy quickly told Sesame what had happened.

"I wonder if it was Morbrecia?" said Sesame, grimly. "She knows we're after the charms. Remember last time we were here? She was going to throw us to the skreels!"*

"You're right!" said Maddy.

"We'll stick together from now on," said Sesame. "The sooner we find another charm the better."

As they started up Lantern Hill, they heard the bell strike one.

They followed the road past houses with roofs of brightly coloured glass, which sparkled like jewels in the bright, wintry sun. Everywhere there were happy Karismans enjoying the new holiday Queen Charm had decreed. But neither of them noticed the shadowy figure of Morbrecia prowling after them.

As they climbed the hill, Sesame told Maddy about

* * * * * * * * * * * * * * * * * * * * * * * * * * *

* Skreel – small flesh-eating fish

208

her meeting with the fairy, Quilla. In a while, they came to the entrance of a park and ahead lay several pathways.

"Which path?" said Maddy.

"That one," said Sesame, choosing a path that wound between trees, strung with lanterns. As they went, they kept a sharp look-out for charms.

"I've forgotten which ones are missing," said Maddy, peering under a bush.

Sesame knew them all by heart and reeled them off easily.

"There's a key, coin, cat and clover," she began. "Moon, lantern, star – that's seven – a dolphin, butterfly, shell and snowflake."

Maddy moaned.

"They could be anywhere," she said.

"We'll find them," said Sesame, confidently. "Sesame Brown will track them down!"

They carried on up the hill and when they were near the top, Sesame felt a tingle at the back of her neck. She felt her locket. Yes! There it was again. Sesame looked around and saw the crest of the hill was covered with enormous crystalline rocks, speckled pink and white. Some balanced precariously, one on top of the other; some lay tilting crazily, as if a giant had flung them there in a tantrum.

A twinkling light caught Sesame's eye. The biggest rock was topped with a lantern; the light inside was flashing and, in her imagination, Sesame thought the beacon was sending her a signal.

"Let's try up there," she said to Maddy. "We might be lucky."

They clambered over boulders, smoothed by wind and weather. It wasn't easy; there were only a few craggy places to hold, but, at last, they reached the beacon. They were walking round it when, all of a sudden, Maddy tripped.

"Ooops!" she cried, falling flat on her face.

"You OK?" said Sesame, helping her up.

"Yeah," said Maddy. "I must've—"

Sesame was already pointing to something, half-buried in the ground.

"You fell over this," she said, scraping away some dirt. She revealed a block of stone.

"It looks like a step," said Maddy.

Then Sesame spotted more steps, leading to a yawning hole in the rock.

"There's a cave!" she exclaimed.

Maddy groaned, remembering the one they'd found in Cornwall.

"No more caves, Ses!" she said. "Anyway, I'm cold enough already. I bet it's freezing in there."

"Come on," pleaded Sesame. "Just a quick look? Promise." And she gave Maddy their secret hand sign.

= True. I'll keep my word!

Reluctantly, Maddy followed Sesame inside. As she did, she thought she heard soft footfalls behind her. But when she turned to look, there was nothing there.

To Sesame and Maddy's surprise, the cave felt strangely warm. A pinkish light pulsed – bright then dim – as if the cave itself was transmitting a glow. Sesame went ahead, searching and searching for a charm she was sure they would find. The further they went, the warmer it became. Suddenly, Maddy felt a blast of hot air above her head and gave a startled shout.

"What's up?" said Sesame, wheeling round.

"The-there," stammered Maddy, pointing to a ledge.

They were looking at a mass of fierce-looking bugs, every one of them breathing fire! By chance, the girls had disturbed some drakons, who had settled there after their attack on Zorgan.

Sesame gulped.

"They don't seem pleased to see us," she quipped.

Maddy backed away.

"Time to go, Ses," she said. "Like, now!"

"R-i-g-h-t," said Sesame, her eyes fixed on the terrifying insects. The bugs were getting madder by the minute, flapping their wings and spitting fire. Slowly she began to edge towards Maddy then stopped suddenly.

She'd spotted something small and silver, glistening on the ledge.

"Maddy, wait!" she hissed. "There's something up there. See? Next to that big bug?"

"No! I'm not looking," said Maddy, her voice trembling with fear. "I don't care what it is. Come on, Ses. We've got to get out of here!"

But Sesame ignored her friend. She stood on tip-toe and stretched out her arm to reach the ledge. The nearest drakon thought she was going to attack and aimed a fiery jet at her.

"Ouch!" yelled Sesame, snatching back her hand to blow on her sore fingers. Flattening herself against the wall she tried again, feeling along the ledge until, at last, her fingers closed around a small, metal object. Clasping it tightly, she and Maddy ran from the cave.

"Phew!" said Maddy. "Those bugs were the scariest!"

"I know," Sesame said, opening her palm. "But it was worth it. Look. I've found another charm!"

"The shell!" Maddy gasped, her eyes wide with delight. "Well done, Ses."

Sesame held up the precious little charm. The sun was setting and the girls watched it glisten in the evening glow. It was beautiful.

But even as they stood there, a shadow fell across their path. Sesame and Maddy squealed with fright. It was the woman in the mask.

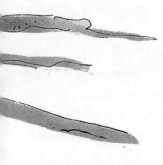

# Eight

It all happened so quickly. One moment Sesame was holding the shell and the next, she wasn't. Morbrecia's skinny arm shot out and snatched the charm from her hand.

"Thank you!" said Morbrecia, sarcastically. "This is mine. Mine, d'you hear? Every one of the charms belongs to ME!"

"No!" cried Sesame, struggling to her feet.

"Vermy Outworlder!" snarled Morbrecia. "You dare to challenge me? *Princess* Morbrecia! Out of my way!" And she pushed Sesame back with her boot.

"Give it back!" cried Maddy fiercely, and made a grab for Morbrecia's ankle. But she was too late. Morbrecia stepped nimbly aside and made off with the charm.

"After her!" yelled Sesame.

And they ran as they'd never run before. But Morbrecia ran even faster – scarily fast – her long black hair streaming in the wind. And before they knew it, they were out of the park and pelting down the road after the fleeing princess.

"We'll never catch her," panted Maddy.

"Come on," said Sesame. "We can't let her get away. We must get the charm back."

But as Morbrecia raced on her way, a child pulling

a toy dragon ran in front of her . . .

"Blatz!"★ cried Morbrecia, as she went head-over-heels. "Ugh!" she groaned, as she landed in an enormous puddle. "AAAAARH!" she screamed, as the charm flew out of her hand and rolled, just out of reach.

Sesame saw her chance and dived for the charm.

"Got it!" she cried, her heart thumping. She clasped the shell tightly in her fist and put it in her pocket.

"Wicked!" said Maddy, giggling at Morbrecia in the puddle.

"Oh, help!" cried Sesame. "Morbrecia's up again. Run!"

And the bell struck two.

* * * * * * * * * * * * * * * * * * * * * * * * * * *

★ **Blatz** – a really angry exclamation

A merry carnival procession was wending its way through the town. Sesame and Maddy dodged in and out of floats, fire-eaters and torch-bearers in their efforts to escape from Morbrecia. She looked mad with rage as she chased after them.

As a magnificent horse-drawn carriage came along, the Charmseekers had to leap aside. It was carrying none other than Queen Charm! She was proudly wearing the Crown of Agapogo and waving to the crowds.

For a split-second, Sesame thought the queen looked straight at her! Could she sense the power of the charm so near? Next thing she knew, Maddy was tugging at her arm.

"Look," she said, pointing to a spectacular dragon train. "Let's hide."

"Good idea," said Sesame.

The girls slipped under the scaly canopy and joined the line of Karisman children, who were supporting the dragon train above their heads.

"Quisto!" exclaimed a very surprised Karisman boy, running in the line.

"Don't mind us," said Maddy. "Just pretend we're not here—"

And Sesame suddenly remembered the Vanishing Cream. *"You may need this sooner than you think!"* Quilla had told her. Well, she needed it right now!

# Nine

"Will it hurt?" whispered Maddy, nervously. "Quilla didn't say," said Sesame, keeping her voice low. "We'll just have to put it on and see."

The dragon train had come to an abrupt halt and Sesame had just told Maddy about the Vanishing Cream. Morbrecia was close and cursing. It was only a matter of seconds before she discovered them. They had to act fast. Sesame opened the pot.

"Me first," said Maddy, bravely.

"Oh, Maddy!" whispered Sesame. "Supposing we never see each other again? You're my best friend!"

"And you're mine," said Maddy, giving Sesame a hug. "The bestest ever! But we've got to get away from Morbrecia, right?"

Sesame nodded. She held out the pot and watched anxiously as Maddy put a blob of bright blue cream on her finger.

"Here goes!" she said, rubbing it into her cheeks. She felt a bit wobbly, then *Ping!*

"Did it work?" said Maddy's voice nearby.

"Um . . . almost," said Sesame. "I can still see your feet."

"Oh, no!" wailed Maddy. "I didn't put enough—"
She stopped.

"Ses!" she cried. "Morbrecia's behind you!"

Morbrecia made a lunge for Sesame. But Sesame ducked, slapped on the cream and *Pop!*
She disappeared before Morbrecia's eyes.

Leaping out of the dragon, the two almost invisible Charmseekers had to find their way back to the gate. They wove their way through a milling crowd of revellers and carnival floats. Maddy swerved round a stilt-walker to avoid a nasty collision; Sesame tripped over an excited dog, which barked furiously at its invisible assailant. But when they paused to catch their breath, they noticed with horror that the Vanishing Cream was wearing off and Morbrecia was not far behind. She screeched with glee when she caught sight of the Charmseekers again.

"Come on," gasped Sesame. "There's Feenix. One last sprint and we're there."

Morbrecia was after them, in full cry, and above her curses they heard the bell CLANG.

"Hurry! Hurry!" cried Feenix, fluttering up and down. The bell clanged twice. "One more strike and the gate shuts!"

As the bell struck three, the Charmseekers threw themselves through the closing gate. Morbrecia flung herself at Sesame but she was too late.
All Sesame left behind was a shoe.

# Spotted on Lantern Hill!

Can you spot 10 things the Charmseekers saw?

☆

Spotted paper lantern
Firecracker
Pot of vanishing cream
Bell
Drakon
Shell
Toy dragon with one wing
Crown of Agapogo
Sesame's lost shoe
Morbrecia's mask

☆

☆ ☆

☆

☆

"I got dumped!" said a cheerful voice. "Nearly lost the board. Fantastic wave. Did you see?"

Sesame and Maddy looked up and saw Nic grinning at them.

"Er, I did, Mr Brown," said Maddy, in a daze. She sat up and brushed sand from her knees.

"Mmm," murmured Sesame vaguely, and scrambled to her feet. "Bad luck, Dad."

Little did he know that they'd just been dumped too! Sesame wasn't sure how they'd got back to the beach, but here they were.

Later, when they were alone in their room at Cliff Cottage, Sesame opened her jewellery box. She took the tiny silver shell from her pocket. But before she put it away, they sat for a while looking at it.

"It's so pretty," said Maddy, admiring the way the charm seemed to shimmer with a light of its own. "No wonder Morbrecia was so keen to have it."

Sesame remembered the awful moment Morbrecia had snatched it from her.

"She's scary," she said.

Maddy shivered at the thought of her.

"I bet she's hopping mad we got away," she said.

"Hey! I'm the one hopping around here," said Sesame, wiggling her toes. "Morbrecia grabbed my flip-flop, remember? Gran gave me a really funny look when I said I didn't know how I'd lost it. She knows when I'm fibbing!"

"Isn't it time you told her?" said Maddy. "About Karisma? Everything?"

"I can't, not yet," said Sesame. "She'd only worry or think I was sickening for something. And Dad would think I was making it up."

Maddy nodded. She understood how crazy their adventures would sound. Who would believe them? Sesame placed the little shell in her jewellery box. It gave them both a sense of wonder and achievement to see it now, lying with the bracelet and the heart and horseshoe charms. They were as real as real could be.

"It's our special secret, Maddy," she said. "We're Charmseekers! We must find all the charms, no matter who tries to stop us. I won't give up 'til I've found every one and returned them to Queen Charm."

Sesame snapped the lid shut.

"I can't wait to go back!" she said.

# Ten

"Agapogo Day was a great success, Your Majesty," said the Silversmith. "The fireworks on Lantern Hill were spectacular. Fit for a dragon!"

"Yes," said Charm, taking off the Crown of Agapogo and placing it on a velvet cushion. "I shall wear this every year on Agapogo Day. From now on Agapogo will always be remembered for giving us the—"

She broke off. The last time she'd seen the Silversmith only one drop of silver remained of the Silver Pool.

The Silversmith smiled, her eyes twinkling.

"All is well," she said, softly. "Zorgan's wretched curse was broken. I took the last drop of silver and cast it into the magic pool. It will take time, but the magic pool will be restored. If we are careful, we shall have sufficient silver for all our needs."

"Spallah!"* exclaimed Charm. "There's only one thing that could please me more. Do you have any news of my charms?"

* * * * * * * * * * * * * * * * * * * * * * * * *

*Spallah – excellent, a triumphant expression

"Indeed I do," said the Silversmith. "One was found this very day! I believe our Charmseeker, Sesame, has it safely in the Outworld."

Charm clapped her hands with delight. "That is marvellous!" she exclaimed.

"Sesame and her friend were at Lantern Hill," said the Silversmith. "Feenix the gatekeeper was boasting about the Charmseekers coming through her gate. Apparently they had a narrow escape—"

The Silversmith bit her tongue. She hadn't meant to let that slip!

"Escape?" said Charm, sounding concerned. "Were the Charmseekers in danger?"

"Probably gossip . . ." began the Silversmith. But Charm was looking at her so intently, she found herself telling the queen everything she knew. Some Karismans had recognised Morbrecia chasing two Outworlders through Lantern Hill that day. Charm listened but with every word her heart grew heavier.

"My sister . . ." she said, quietly. "Can this be true? Is Morbrecia after the charms?"

"It seems so, Your Majesty," said the Silversmith.

Now Charm knew what the Silversmith had feared all along.

"So Morbrecia stole my bracelet!" she said. Her eyes opened wide with horror as she recalled that terrible night. "My sister was the SPIDER!"

230

Alone in her workshop once more, the Silversmith reflects on all that has happened. Of the thirteen magic candles, one more has flickered and gone out. It is the candle that bears the name of the little shell. Now ten candles glow and each will burn brightly until its missing charm is found. She knows Sesame will return soon. She has chosen well. Sesame won't give up, until her quest is over.

But she fears for her special Charmseeker. Zorgan will do his best to thwart Sesame's mission and Morbrecia will stop at nothing to recover the charms. Oh! There is such bitterness in Morbrecia's heart, such jealousy of her sister, Charm.

But that is another story. It must be told another day!

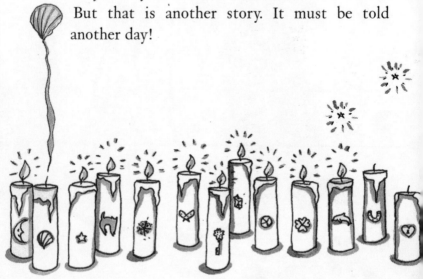

*Acknowledgements*

The *Charmseekers* books would not have been written without the support and encouragement of my friends and family. To these many I owe a great debt of gratitude.

I would especially like to thank my publisher Fiona Kennedy for her faith in believing I could write way beyond my own expectations. Her creative, tactful and skilful editing kept me on the right track and helped me write a better story. I am also grateful to Julia and Eliza Spindel, Olivia Camsey, Ghiselle and Isadora Green for taking part in my research, and to my cousin Dodie Houston, a teacher, for her valuable advice.

Finally a million thanks go to my husband, Tom, for his inexhaustible patience, critical appraisal, comfort and help along the way; and to my daughters Abigail and Imogen, for their unfailing love and enthusiastic support.

Amy Tree

Join me, Sesame Brown, in the magical
world of Karisma – and you can be
a Charmseeker too!

For more about the books, regular
Charmseeker updates, fun and games,
and everything you ever wanted to know
about Sesame Brown and her friends, visit

www.charmseekers.co.uk

Join the Charmseekers

at

www.Charmseekers.co.uk

Join the Charmseekers

at

www.Charmseekers.co.uk